P9-CFW-309

THE THIRD FIGURE

Also by Collin Wilcox

THE BLACK DOOR

The Third Figure

COLLIN WILCOX

DODD, MEAD & COMPANY

NEW YORK

RED BADGE
MYSTERY

Library of Congress Catalog Card Number: 68-15410

Printed in the United States of America
by Vail-Ballou Press, Inc., Binghamton, N.Y.

This book is dedicated to Lelia

THE THIRD FIGURE

1

I PROPPED my feet on the coffee table and idly gazed out on my own private vista, that portion of the San Francisco night visible through an oversize plate glass window dominating one wall of my living room. On the first of each month I was sometimes acutely aware of the price I paid for the view, yet I never really regretted the extravagance. On a clear night, from the east slope of Telegraph Hill, any price seemed worthwhile.

It was eight twenty. She was twenty minutes late.

Perhaps, after all, she wouldn't come. It had happened before: an anonymous phone call, arranging a fictitious appointment.

If she didn't come by nine, I decided, I'd go to a movie. It was Friday night, after all. And even though I had nothing specially planned, it seemed a shame to—

The doorbell sounded, sharp and startling. Hastily I rose to my feet, crossed to the door and softly swung open the cover of the wide-angle scanner. I saw an oddly assorted couple standing in the dim light. The woman was middle-aged, plainly dressed, dumpy and dowdy. At her side stood a small, misshapen man whose head barely reached his companion's shoulder. If the woman's clothes were nondescript, the man's clothes were almost flamboyantly stylish. As I opened the door I was wondering whether dwarfs habitually dressed in bold patterns, perhaps as a gesture of defiance.

The woman was the first to speak.

"Mr. Drake? Mr. Stephen Drake?" Her voice was low and quiet.

"Yes." I stepped back, gesturing for them to enter. "You're . . . ?"

Not replying, she walked into the room, followed by the misshapen man. Watching her, it seemed as if her manner had something of the European peasant's stolid, suspicious self-sufficiency. Her face, too, had the flat planes and olive hue of the southern European.

After a brief, calm scrutiny of my living room, she turned to face me. Her eyes were dark; her gaze was speculative and calculating as she said, "My name is Mrs. Aidia Vennezio." She paused, as if expecting some special reaction. She was watching me closely.

A little disconcerted by her opaquely appraising eyes, I bobbed my head in greeting.

"How do you do?" I replied, feeling faintly foolish. "Won't you sit down?" I gestured to a nearby sofa.

"Thank you." She nodded politely, and moved to the sofa. As she did, she also nodded to the dwarf and moved her head toward the door. Without a word the small man crossed the room and let himself out.

Surprised, I chose an armchair facing her.

Where had the dwarf gone? Would he be back? Irrelevantly, perhaps, I tried to remember whether I'd left the door on the latch.

2

I watched my guest settling herself on the sofa. She sat precisely in the center, with both hands holding her bulky black leather purse on her lap. She wore a coat made of heavy blue cloth. Her dress was a darker blue; her shoes were serviceable black. Her graying hair was pulled back in a bun. She seemed to be in her late forties or early fifties, and somehow she reminded me of a cleaning woman who'd worked hard, saved every penny and now sat with her life's savings stuffed into her black leather handbag.

Yet there was something more to Mrs. Vennezio—something strangely inflexible and inscrutable.

And there was the dwarf, dismissed with a small, practiced nod.

I cleared my throat. "Would you like something to drink, Mrs. Vennezio? Coffee?"

She shook her head. Then, without preamble, she said abruptly, "You're Mr. Drake the clairvoyant, aren't you?"

I sighed, then nodded. The question always disconcerted me, no matter how it was put. I always had the feeling that most people thought of clairvoyant as synonymous with charlatan. Or faker. Or worse.

"I read about you." She seemed to expect a reply, but I could think of none. Then, in the small silence that followed, she seemed to come to a decision. Her mouth tightened and her chin came up. Her voice hinted at a quiet defiance as she said:

"I'm Mrs. Dominic Vennezio. You've probably heard about my husband."

"Dom—" I swallowed, looking at her with what I realized was transparent amazement. "Dominic *Vennezio?*

3

The . . . the . . ." I groped for the word.

Her dark eyes never wavered as she answered, "The gangster. Yes."

Vividly, I could still see the headlines: *Crime Czar Slain in Beach Hideaway. Dominic Vennezio Murdered in Secret Love Nest.*

Dominic Vennezio, the Syndicate's man in California —the overlord of crime in Southern California—a member in good standing of organized crime's ruling council. It had been less than a month since the murder. And now, in my own living room, the widow sat in her plain blue coat. Watching me. Waiting.

Did she want me to help her? It had been a gangland slaying. To find the murderer would mean a Mafia death sentence, beyond the slightest doubt.

"I'm sorry, Mrs. Vennezio," I said lamely. "I know it must've been a—a terrible shock for you. Your husband's murder, I mean."

She didn't reply. There was something in her implacable silence that made me ill at ease. Or perhaps it was her dark, expressionless eyes, never leaving my own. I realized that I was shifting uncomfortably in my chair.

"You're a crime reporter, too," she said in the same abrupt voice. "Is that right?"

I nodded. "Yes. That's how I got into—into clairvoyance in the first place. In looking into crimes, you see, I discovered that—"

"Then you know about Dominic," she interrupted. "You probably even wrote about him, in the newspaper."

"Well, yes, I have. But—"

"You know about the Outfit, then."

"The Syndicate, you mean?"

4

She shrugged. "Call it whatever you want to. But you know what I mean."

"Yes," I answered in a low voice. "Yes, I know what you mean."

"Good." She nodded, as if satisfied. Then, deliberately, she said, "My husband wasn't murdered by the Outfit, Mr. Drake. Everyone thinks so, but he wasn't."

"But . . ." I shrugged, then helplessly shook my head. There was nothing I could say. It was a certainty that Dominic Vennezio's murderer would never be prosecuted in the normal course of events. Surely she didn't expect me to find Vennezio's murderer, turn him over to the police and then calmly wait for a bullet in the head.

"It wasn't the Outfit," she repeated. "I know it wasn't."

"That's just your opinion, Mrs. Vennezio. I'm sure they wouldn't admit it to you if they'd killed him. They'd probably be afraid you'd—"

"They aren't afraid of anything," she interrupted in a low, tight voice. "You're a crime reporter. You know I'm right. If they aren't afraid of the police, why should they be afraid of me?"

"Still, assuming they had him killed, you couldn't expect them to admit it to you, could you? Any more than you'd expect them to admit it to the police—or to anyone else, for that matter. It doesn't mean they're foolish, just because they aren't afraid."

"They'd admit it to me," she said doggedly.

"But why? Why would they admit it to you, when they wouldn't admit it to anyone else? It's not logical."

"They'd admit it to me because they've been trying to make up their minds for two years whether to kill me. So, if they killed Dom, the first thing they'd do is tell me

5

about it, as a warning. About half the time they kill someone, it's a warning to someone else, too." She said it matter-of-factly, as if discussing the tactics of an unscrupulous loan shark. Something about her monotonous, uninflected voice, with its trace of an old-country accent, gave a chilling weight to her words. There was a kind of stoic resignation in her manner, too—as if she didn't really care whether they killed her or not.

"Do they know you've come to me, Mrs. Vennezio?" I asked.

"They know everything."

"Let me put it differently, then, Do they *approve* of you coming to me?"

"If they didn't approve, I wouldn't be here. I'd be with Dom."

"Yes, but that—that's another assumption you're making, Mrs. Vennezio. How can you be sure— absolutely sure—they know you're here? They aren't omnipotent you know. They have their contacts, I admit. But they're not—"

"Reggie tells them." She moved her head toward the plate glass window. "The one that came in with me. Reggie Fay. It's his job."

"Do you mean that it's his responsibility to report everything you do to the Outfit?"

She nodded.

"But why?"

"I already told you: because they've been trying to decide whether to kill me or not. For two years, now."

Feeling a sense of baffled frustration, I looked at her for a long moment before finally saying, "I'm sorry, Mrs. Vennezio, but none of this makes any sense to me. If

6

we're going to get anywhere, you're going to have to tell me the whole story, from the beginning. Otherwise, there's no point in our—"

"I moved out on Dominic just about two years ago," she said in her expressionless voice. "He started playing around with another woman, and I moved out."

"And Dominic Vennezio let you go?" I was surprised. The Syndicate's first concern is for the probity of its leaders. The executives of organized crime live more proscribed lives than their counterparts in big business. Divorce, perhaps, was tolerated. But never a scandal.

"I wanted to leave him," she said, "and I did. There wasn't anything he could do about it."

"But—"

"Before I did it, I first of all wrote down things I know. Things about Dominic. I made four copies and put two of them in two separate safe-deposit boxes and gave the other two to different lawyers. And I told Dom that if anything happened to me, those letters would go to four different people: the President, J. Edgar Hoover, the governor of California and the head of the California Crime Commission."

I thought about it for a moment before saying, "From what I've heard of the Outfit, Mrs. Vennezio, I don't think those four letters would've permanently stopped them if they really wanted you dead. Something like this happened several years ago, and they simply tortured the man until he told them where the incriminating material was hidden. Then the man turned up dead."

"But Dominic would never've let them do that" she answered doggedly. "He wanted his freedom, all right." But not that bad. Besides, I never told anyone else about

7

those letters. **Only Dominic.**"

"You just finished saying, though, that they knew everything. You also said they've been considering murdering you for two years. So they must have known."

She thought about it, then indifferently shrugged my mere logic aside. "Maybe so. I was only talking about Dominic. But he's not the only one, you know. The others, back East, they tell him what to do. Besides, the way I felt when I moved out, I didn't care whether they killed me or not. Maybe Dominic did, but I didn't."

"Did he still have some feeling for you, then, when you moved out? Is that what you mean?"

"We were married thirty years and we had two kids. Even someone like Dominic, he don't forget things like that."

"What kind of a man was he, Mrs. Vennezio? Aside from this—this indiscretion, what kind of a man was he?"

Her hands tightened on her handbag and her voice dropped to a huskier note as she said, "Dominic was a good man—a good husband. In his business, he was hard on people. It's all he knew; it's the way he learned. But he never treated me mean. Even after he met that—that woman, he never treated me mean. It just happened to him like it happened to a lot of men when they start getting old. They start wondering about their manhood, and once they start wondering they can't stop. Most of the time, with Dominic, it was a girl he'd find on a trip. He had to go back East every six months or so, for meetings. And he'd find himself a girl, and that would be that. I—I knew about it. I never said anything, but I knew. But this thing—this woman, that was something else. He paid her

rent, and everything. And bought her a car. And—
and . . ." Her voice trailed off. For the first time she
lowered her eyes.

"What about a divorce?"

Slowly she shook her head.

"We're Catholic. Both of us. Besides, we—we'd been
together for thirty years. That's a long time."

I thought about it before deciding to say, "Let me ask
you this, Mrs. Vennezio: If I were able to find out who
murdered your husband, what would you do with the
information?"

She raised her eyes. "That'd depend on who did it. I
just want to know. I've *got* to know. And no one will tell
me anything."

"Have you gone to the police?"

"No." She seemed almost primly shocked, as if I'd suggested a gross impropiety. After thirty years as the wife
of a mafisio, I reflected, it wasn't surprising.

"It's the Outfit, then, who won't tell you. Is that
right?"

She nodded, once more dropping her eyes. And now
she sighed deeply. For the first time I realized how much
it must be costing her to talk so candidly about her husband's transgressions. And with the realization, I felt a
small pang of guilt. I was titillating my curiosity, with no
real intention of doing as she asked. So, as gently as I
could, I said:

"I can't help you, Mrs. Vennezio. You must know that.
You say the Outfit didn't have him killed, but that's just
another assumption you're making. If you're wrong and I
go sniffing around, I'll find myself in the river. Besides,
even if they didn't kill him, they probably don't want

anyone sniffing around."

For perhaps a full half-minute she stared at me, and during the interval I saw her eyes harden and her mouth tighten. Watching her, I realized that the image of the cleaning woman had faded, replaced by that of an Italian peasant woman in her ritual black shawl, stolid and silently long-suffering—yet capable of a hot-eyed, white-knuckled passion.

She was rummaging now in her handbag. I was aware of a little lift of excitement as I realized she was counting money. Finally she neatly tapped together a small sheaf of bills, which she placed on the coffee table before her.

"There's one thing I learned from Dominic," she said evenly, "and it's that everyone has his price." She pointed to the stack of bills. "That's a thousand dollars, Mr. Drake. It's not for finding Dom's murderer. It's just for taking the time to go down and see Frankie Russo. He's the man who's taking over Dominic's job. That's all I ask: just take the thousand dollars, and talk to Russo. If he doesn't want you around, he'll tell you, and you'll still have the thousand dollars. If he says you can help me—" she lifted a thicker sheaf of bills from inside her handbag "—there's nine thousand dollars more if you can find out who murdered Dominic."

I swallowed. Twice.

"But what'll you do with the information, assuming I can find the murderer for you? You can't go to the police, especially if someone from the Outfit is involved. Not unless you want to spend the rest of your life locked up in protective custody."

She didn't answer the question directly, but instead said, "I've already told you, I have to know." She glanced almost contemptuously around my living room before saying quietly, "You didn't come from the old country, Mr. Drake. Probably your folks didn't either—or even your grandparents. But I was born in Sicily. I can still remember it, living there. And Sicilians never forget it, when something like this happens. We . . ." She shrugged, then shook her head. Plainly she herself didn't understand the dim, almost primitive instincts driving her. In a lower, baffled voice she said, "I just can't think of anything else, Mr. Drake. I've just got to know who killed him. It—it's all I care about. It's all I think about, anymore. When it first happened, I thought I didn't care. I even thought I was glad, when I first heard about it. I—I started laughing, and I couldn't stop. Then I realized that I was really crying. I thought I'd got my revenge, but I was wrong. And now I can't think about anything but finding out who killed him. Maybe it's something bad I'm doing. The priest says it is. But I . . ."

She stared down at her handbag, blinking rapidly. "Please help me, Mr. Drake. I can't go to the police, and I can't go to a private detective, except the crooked ones. When I read about you, I just—just thought you were the only one who could help me. I guess maybe I'm superstitious. When I was a little girl, I used to think I could see things, like you do. I used to think I could see the Virgin, and I used to talk to her. I was even examined once by four priests, like they used to examine saints. So when I heard about you, I . . ." Her voice trailed off. As she sat with head bowed, fiddling fretfully with the clasp of her handbag, the image of the vindictive peasant woman faded, along with that of the humble cleaning

11

woman. She was simply a grieving middle-aged house-wife, sitting forlornly on my sofa.

I looked at the small pile of bills on the coffee table—a thousand dollars, for taking a trip to Los Angeles. I would be a thousand dollars richer, just for talking with Frankie Russo—and for obeying his instructions not to help Mrs. Vennezio find her husband's murderer. It was, I realized, a cynical calculation. Yet, almost beyond doubt, that's the way it would happen.

And, besides the money, there was the professional advantage of actually contacting a member of the Mafia elite. Few crime reporters ever got the opportunity.

There seemed little risk, yet it was difficult to be sure. I'd been a crime reporter for five years, and I knew the vast power organized crime could wield. True, most reporters had a certain immunity, as did most police officers. But private investigators weren't always so lucky. As for clairvoyants . . .

I sighed and lit a cigarette. There could be no harm in hearing her story.

"Tell me about it, Mrs. Vennezio. Tell me everything that happened."

She raised her head.

"You'll do it, then?" She didn't smile, nor did her voice betray any emotion.

"I might. Tell me, though, what happened. Start with your husband's relationship with this woman."

She drew a deep breath, then took the purse from her lap and placed it on the couch beside her. She clasped her hands and gazed off across the room. Something in her slow, wooden speech and tightly clasped hands reminded me of the confessional. This was how she must sound to her priest, I was thinking.

"It all started almost two and a half years ago," she was saying. "Dom hired this—this woman away from someone else. She was working for one of the real estate companies that Dom used. Dom was very interested in real estate. He was always buying and selling houses and apartment houses. So then, one day, he told me that he was going to start his own real estate business. He said it'd make him a lot of money if he had his own real estate office."

"This was his own private business," I interrupted. "It had nothing to do with the Syndicate."

"That's right, just his own. But really, see, it was all a—a front, to get this woman to work for him. I heard later that he offered her twice the salary she was getting."

"What's her name?"

"Faith Hanson." She pronounced it with difficulty.

"Did she have a husband?"

"Her husband drank, I think."

"Children?"

She nodded. "She has a boy. A teen-ager."

"Was she actually a real estate broker?"

"No. She was just a secretary. Dom hired a broker, too. And before they were done, they had three or four salesmen working, too. It turned out to be a good business. I have to give Dom that: he could make money. Even on the square."

"And this real estate business was on the square?"

She nodded.

"Do you think Dominic had been seeing this woman before he hired her?"

Again she nodded. "They'd been seeing each other for two, three months."

"Then what happened, after she went to work for him?"

"Well, they—they started seeing each other all the time. It got so, once a week, Dom wouldn't come home. He'd always say it was business, but we both knew he was lying. So, one day, I asked him right out whether he was keeping another woman."

"Did he admit it?"

"Yes."

"What explanation did he give?"

"He just said that he loved her, and couldn't help himself. It didn't have anything to do with me, he said. He still loved me, he kept saying. It was just that he couldn't help himself."

"How old is this Hanson woman, Mrs. Vennezio?"

"She's about forty."

"And how old was Dominic?"

"He's—he was fifty-nine."

"What about her husband? What happened to him?"

"He drank, like I said, but that's all I know—except that, just after Faith Hanson went to work for Dominic, her husband disappeared."

"You mean . . ." I didn't quite know how to put it.

"No, it wasn't like that, I don't think. I never knew, but I don't think it was like that. I'd've heard."

"Was the husband ever seen again?"

"I don't know. I don't think so."

I sat for a long moment regarding her—trying to decide whether she was evading the question. In assessing her mannerisms, it was difficult to separate guilt from

14

embarrassment.

"You've got to tell me everything, Mrs. Vennezio," I said finally. "Otherwise I can't help you."

"I know."

"And you're certain Dominic didn't—do away with Mr. Hanson?"

"I don't know one way or the other. I told you."

"What about Mrs. Hanson's son? Is he living with her?"

"He lived with her for a year. But then, last year, she sent him to a private school. One of those fancy schools in the Ojai Valley."

"When the boy left, did Dominic actually move in with the Hanson woman?"

"No."

"Why not?"

"They wouldn't't've liked that."

"The Outfit, you mean?"

She nodded.

"But Dominic was the head man down South," I prodded. "He was the one that made the rules."

She looked at me briefly before saying, "Dom used to say that the higher you got, the closer they watch you. And it's true. There were a dozen guys out for his job. Everything he did wrong, it got back East."

"Did they know about his romance with Mrs. Hanson, back East?"

"Sure they did."

"And they didn't mind?"

"Not as long as he used his head and didn't get out of line."

"And did he use his head?"

15

She didn't reply. As she'd been talking, her gathering tension was more and more evident. Still, I needed information.

"How did the actual murder occur?" I asked. "Tell me everything you know about it—especially anything that might not've got into the papers."

For a moment I thought she hadn't heard me, or didn't intend to reply. She simply sat staring off across the room, her lips pressed into a tight, painful line.

"How did it actually happen, Mrs. Vennezio? If I'm going to help you, I've got to know. Tell it to me from the beginning."

She was silent for a moment. Then, haltingly, she began to speak. "He'd gone to the beachhouse. It used to be our beachhouse. They—they spent weekends there. And that's when it—it happened. On Sunday night."

"Was Faith Hanson with him when he got killed?"

"She got there just afterward. She found him."

"Was she questioned by the police?"

"Yes."

"What did she say?"

"Just that she walked in and found him lying in the living room, dead. Shot."

"Did the police think that Dominic knew his murderer?"

She nodded. "They think he let him in."

"How did the police learn about the murder?"

"A phone call."

"Anonymous?"

"Yes."

"Man or woman?"

"A man, the papers said."

16

"Did your husband usually have a bodyguard with him?"

"Usually. But not—not on weekends."

"Who did the police question?"

"Everyone. They put on a good show."

"What do you mean by that, Mrs. Vennezio?"

She hesitated before saying, "We live in La Palada. Do you know anything about La Palada, Mr. Drake?"

I did, but I wanted to hear what she'd say. So I shook my head and waited for her to continue.

"There's only three thousand people in La Palada," she said. "It's right outside Los Angeles, but it's a separate town. It's incorporated, and everything. It's where most of the big shots live, and it's got the lowest crime rate in the whole state."

"The big shots from the Outfit, you mean."

"Yes."

"And they own the town, including the police."

"Yes."

"Did the police turn up a suspect, as part of the show they put on?"

"No. They just questioned a lot of people, and made a big noise for the papers. Then, after a couple of weeks, it all died down. No one really expected anything different. It's like when Bugsy Siegel got killed. No one ever expected the murderer would get caught. And he never was."

"Yet you still insist your husband wasn't killed by someone in organized crime?" I asked incredulously.

"I'm not saying that, Mr. Drake. There were probably fifty men who would've liked to see Dominic dead, for

17

different reasons. Anyone makes enemies, no matter what business he's in, and Dom made his share. Maybe more than his share. What I'm telling you, though, is that his murder wasn't ordered. Siegel's murder was ordered, but not Dominic's. The Outfit didn't—"

"Everyone I've ever talked to about the murder thought it was a professional job," I interrupted. "And that includes several policemen."

She moved her clasped hands fretfully before her.

"Talk to Russo, Mr. Drake. That's all I'm asking you to do. Go down to La Palada and talk to him."

"Will he talk to me, do you think?"

She nodded.

"How can you be so sure, Mrs. Vennezio?"

"I made a bargain with him."

"What kind of a bargain?"

"The letters—the four letters I wrote. Two days ago, I told Russo about the letters. I said I'd give them to him, if he'd talk to you. And he said he would."

"And you gave them to him?"

She nodded, silent and resigned.

"But—but what's to prevent him killing you?"

"He promised," she said simply.

"And you believed him?"

"Yes, Mr. Drake. I believed him. I made promises, and so did Russo. If we both keep our words, there won't be any trouble. That's the way it's always been, Mr. Drake —for hundreds of years." She reached over for her purse and got to her feet, heavily. She pointed to the small pile of bills on the table between us.

"Take the money, Mr. Drake. Go see Russo. He'll be expecting you. He's in the phone book, and he's expecting you. If you keep your word with him, he's not a bad man. He's like Dominic was. They're just the same."

She turned and walked to the door. Hastily crossing the room, I opened the door for her. I wanted to say something, to comfort her. But she was already outside. I watched her get into a car parked at the curb. As the car pulled away, I saw two men in the front seat.

I closed the door, locked it and walked back into my living room. I picked up the small stack of bills—a thousand dollars, in hundred-dollar bills.

Automatically I took out my wallet and slipped the money inside. As I did, I was conscious of a sudden, chilling sense of forboding. I'd felt it first as I'd watched the car pulling away, with the two figures in the front seat and the single figure in the rear. Remembering the slow progress of the car, it seemed as if the figures inside were part of some strange procession, traveling to some dim and distant place.

2

I AWOKE Saturday morning to a feeling of apprehension. Over coffee, glumly, my thoughts kept returning to the legend of Faust, irrevocably selling his soul to the devil.

By the second cup of coffee I'd decided to write out a check to Mrs. Vennezio for a thousand dollars, mail it and forget it.

An hour later I'd packed, got an airline reservation for later that afternoon and notified my long-suffering city editor that I'd be out of town for a few days.

It was ultimately a reporter's overwhelming curiosity, I realized, that had compelled the decision. Although I'd been lucky enough, over the past few years, to solve a few well-publicized murders by the painful process of groping among the dark and confusing images of my subconscious, yet I was nevertheless primarily a professional crime reporter. Even though my employer's publicity department took great pains to ballyhoo the mysterious methods of their "clairvoyant sleuth-of the mind," it was actually conventional news-gathering techniques that provided me with the disembodied lines and shapes from which, with luck, the final subconscious images unaccountably emerged.

And so, as a newspaperman, I had no choice but to go down to Los Angeles and talk with Frankie Russo. Beyond doubt, I would never be able to write directly about the conversation. Yet, also beyond doubt, I would never be able to forgive myself if I surrendered the opportunity to interview one of the kingpins of organized crime in America.

In the meantime, I had three spare hours. After some deliberation, I decided to try and reach Captain George Larsen, chief of the Detective Bureau's homicide division. A long, laconic Dane with a quick wit and a wry sense of humor, Larsen had been the first police department official to treat me as anything more than a witch doctor disguised in a Harris tweed suit. Later, as we'd come to know each other better, we'd become friends.

Larsen was off duty, and at first I was reluctant to call him at home. Friendship is one thing, Saturday afternoons something else. Yet I was also reluctant to depart for Los Angeles without at least touching base with the law, and an interview with Larsen at home was much more appealing than one at headquarters.

Luckily, Larsen was working on his boat in the garage, and his wife was delivering an angel food cake to her church bazaar. I would therefore be welcome, if I didn't mind inhaling resin fumes and helping with the fiber glass.

And so, shortly after noon, I found myself holding a roll of glass fiber and watching Larsen as he smoothed out a section of freshly applied resin.

"You should open that window," I said, moving my

head toward the back of the garage. "You need some cross-ventilation."

"It won't open. Besides, this is the last I'm going to do. I have to take Carrie downtown as soon as she gets home." He dropped a length of the glass fiber into the resin. "Hand me that squeegee, will you?"

I handed it over, then glanced at my watch. I'd been holding glass fiber and handing over tools for more than a half hour, while waiting my chance to bring up the subject of Dominic Vennezio. But Larsen, muttering constantly about a bad batch of resin that was setting too quickly, had been preoccupied.

Now, finally, he dropped the squeegee into a nearby bucket of solvent.

"Let's go inside and get some coffee," he said, leading the way. "These fumes are something."

I poured the coffee from a pot on the stove while Larsen set out sugar and cream on the small kitchen table

"Well, what can I do for you?" he asked, sipping the coffee and for the first time giving me his full attention.

I paused a moment, conscious of savoring the sensation I was about to produce.

"Dominic Vennezio's widow wants me to find out who killed her husband."

He sipped a small swallow of coffee, set down his cup and examined me appraisingly with his pale blue Nordic eyes.

"You're kidding," he said.

I shook my head. "She came to my place last night and laid it all out. She stayed for more than an hour."

He sighed, perhaps with a certain weariness, perhaps more with a wry regret. Larsen was both an honest and a realistic cop. He realized that corruption existed in municipal politics, and therefore in lawmaking, and therefore in law enforcement. He knew that organized crime was the principal reason. Protection money is the one fixed item of overhead in the budget of every illegal venture. Lasen knew all this—and more. Yet, like most honest cops, he preferred not to think about it, just as a shoe salesman would rather not think of the frequency with which his customers' feet are washed.

"What all did she say?" he asked, his voice noncommittal.

As concisely as I could, I told him.

"And you're going to do it?" he said incredulously.

"This morning, I wasn't. Now I am."

"What changed your mind? The money?" His voice was chilled with irony.

"No, it wasn't just the money. It's the chance to interview Frankie Russo. You know as well as I do that organized crime is the biggest single business in the country. And it's the biggest, most sensational news story in the country, too—in the world, for that matter."

"It's the biggest untold story in the country. Anything you'll ever need for material, you've already got. You don't have to talk to Russo, and you know it." He shifted in his chair, suppressing an impatient pique. "You could spend a week writing news stories that'd never get past your own city desk—or maybe your own wastebasket, once you thought about it."

"I could say the same to you. San Francisco's a clean town as far as organized crime is concerned. It's the only clean big city in the country, outside of maybe Portland and Seattle. But you could still spend that same week arresting a lot of people that you know are guilty as hell."

"Knowing is one thing," he said sharply. "Proving it's something else."

For a long moment we sat staring at each other. I was regretting my last remark; possibly Larsen was regretting his.

Finally he took a deep breath and stirred his coffee, frowning.

"Send the money back, Steve. You've taken your lumps over this clairvoyance thing. I gave you a few myself, a couple of years ago. But this is different. You could find yourself in deep, permanent trouble."

"With the law, you mean?"

"With the law or with the Outfit. Just because Mrs. Vennezio doesn't think her husband was murdered in the, ah, line of duty doesn't make it so."

"But she's got Russo talked into seeing me. That must mean something."

"It probably does. It probably means that Russo wants those letters."

"But . . ."

"I'm telling you, Steve: you can't possibly win. If the murder turns out to be a professional job, done on contract, and you find out who did it, you could be murdered yourself. If it wasn't a professional job, then it's possible Russo might let you go ahead. He doesn't want unauthorized murders in his organization. It's bad business. Sloppy management. However, if you do help him, then you'll be on his side. He'll take your information and use it to enforce 'discipline,' as they call it. You could be an accessory. At the very least, you'll be on his payroll, just the same as if you were one of his lawyers, for in-

24

stance. So then, if you go to the police, you'll be in trouble with Russo. If you don't go to the police, though, you'll be violating the law. So you can't win, no matter which way you jump. It's happened to plenty of people, Steve, believe me. Just last year a vending machine operator walked into a police station and asked for protection, if he'd talk. He said he was scared—that he'd been a legitimate businessman for years, but got into financial difficulty. He couldn't get a loan through regular channels, and finally—rather than lose his business—he took a loan from the Outfit. He didn't know it was the Outfit, but he knew something wasn't quite right, either. That's how it all started—that's how it always starts, with money. Easy money. A year later the Outfit was running his business, using him for a front. So he finally decided to get out. But he made the mistake of telling his story to the wrong cop—a hack lieutenant who decided to talk it over with the D.A.'s office before putting the guy in protective custody. The lieutenant told the guy to come back in the morning. So the guy walked out of the police station, and that's the last anyone saw of him—until his body washed up, a week later."

"But . . ." I moistened my lips. "But I'm working for Mrs. Vennezio, not for Russo. All I have to do is give her the murderer's name. That's the agreement. It's got nothing to do with the Outfit."

In exasperation, Larsen sharply shook his head. "That's being just plain naïve, Steve. If you were a—a society reporter, I could understand it. But you've spent five years reporting crime. You should know better."

"Well . . ." Indecisively I hesitated before deciding to say, "There's the money, too. Ten thousand dollars. I—I was thinking that I could put it in a mutual fund. It could be an annuity."

"I thought you said it wasn't the money."

"It isn't. Not entirely. Still, I'd be a fool not to think about it. Newspapers don't pay that much, George—and the clairvoyance business hasn't been very brisk lately, either. So when you add it all up—"

"When you add it all up," he interrupted, "there's something that doesn't sound right. Mrs. Vennezio moves out on her husband. Supposedly she'd've divorced him, except that she's Catholic. She hasn't lived with him for two years, during which time he's been keeping another woman. Then Vennezio gets murdered. And now his widow can't rest until she knows who murdered him." Larsen shook his head. "It just doesn't make sense, Steve. There's something missing."

"You haven't talked to her, though. She's a—a peasant type. She's superstitious, and she's not really very bright —or at least not very sophisticated. Also, she's a Sicilian, and apparently she was raised to go by either the code of the church or the code of the Mafia, whichever applied. And, in this case, it's the Mafia. Vengeance. She's got to know who—"

"But that's exactly where the whole thing smells. The Mafia has its code of vengeance, all right. God knows there were enough blood feuds, even in this country— and not so long ago, either. But don't forget omerta—the code of silence. No matter what happens, you're not supposed to talk about it—and especially not to the police. Now, you're not exactly the police, but you're not exactly the corner grocer, either. And if Mrs. Vennezio is already in hot water with the Outfit, the last thing she'd do is contact someone on the outside. And you know it, Steve. You're closing your mind to some very obvious points, here. And it could be dangerous. I'm telling you," he repeated, "that you could end up dead, or at the very least beaten silly, just to remind you not to talk. And then, if you don't talk, you could actually be indicted for withholding material evidence in a capital crime."

"Who'd indict me?" I asked.

"What?" His voice was short and irritable. I'd seldom seen Larsen really angry, but now his lips were tightened and his jaw was clenched.

"I said, who'd indict me? The district attorney of La Palada?"

For a moment I thought he was actually going to lose his temper, something I'd never seen. But he simply said, "La Palada," as if it were an obscenity.

"Well, I mean it, George. Who would indict me?"

"You talk like you're on the other side already."

Now I felt myself becoming angry.

"That's a lot of crap, and you know it. I asked the question for a reason. The murder of Dominic Vennezio is already swept under the rug. There'll never be an arrest made, and you realize it as well as I do. Now, if that's the case, why the hell shouldn't I make a few thousand dollars? For that matter, why shouldn't I make myself one thousand dollars, just for going to Los Angeles and getting an interview that any crime reporter in the country would give anything to get? That's all I'm committed to now, you know—just a trip down to Los Angeles. I could be right back here Monday morning."

"You're forgetting one thing."

"I am?"

"Yes, you are. When you talk about it being a closed case, don't forget about the CIIB."

"The what?"

"The Criminal Identification and Investigation Bureau. California's FBI."

"They don't ask for indictments, though." I hesitated. "Do they?"

"Not usually. But they can, in certain situations. And La Palada is a situation they're looking into."

"Well, I know, but . . ."

"There's another thing I'd like to know."

"What's that?" I was aware that I must sound defensive. Suddenly it was the way I felt.

"Why did Mrs. Vennezio come to you?"

"I've already told you, there wasn't anyone else she could go to. Besides, she—she read my clippings."

"Oh."

"Well, what's wrong with that?" Now my voice sounded plaintive—also the way I felt.

"Nothing's wrong with it, ecept that you know as well as I do that you've always worked with the police. You need the information we develop. You've admitted to me, several times, that these—these flashes of yours are a pretty sometimes thing. They're—"

"Now listen, George. You're the one person in the world who should know that—"

"They're genuine flashes, all right," he interrupted smoothly. "I'm not saying they're not. I've profited by them myself, and I've always been the first one to admit it. Publicly. All I'm saying is that you shouldn't become the victim of your own publicity. You know as well as I do that the *Sentinel* hired you for your publicity value when you found that murderer down in San Jose. And you also know that every time you and the San Francisco Police Department managed to come up with a murderer, the *Sentinel* spread your picture all over the front page, thereby selling a few thousand extra papers. Now, I'm not knocking it, Steve. And I'm not knocking you. All I'm pointing out is that, by your own admission, you operate just about like any reasonably talented detective. You pound the pavements, and you spend a lot of time chasing your tail. And then—still by your own statements—after you've walked a few miles and chased down a few bum leads and spent a lot of tlme moping around my office, you finally get your flash. But the point is that you've usually had help. Also, you've sometimes been wrong, and sometimes you've just simply failed. Now . . ." Again he leveled his long forefinger at me. "Now, everyone fails. It's no sin. But if you start messing around with the Outfit and they don't like the way things are going, they don't just call you into the boss's office for a friendly little chat."

I thought about it and then said, "You're contradicting yourself, George."

"How do you mean?" He reached over to the stove for the coffee pot.

"According to what you said first, the thing I have to worry about is what would happen if I found out who killed Vennezio. Now you're worrying what'll happen if I don't. You can't have it both ways."

Larsen refilled his cup, glanced at mine and then shrugged, resigned.

"All right, go ahead. Everyone's entitled to make a damned fool of himself once in a while, and it's obvious you're determined to do just that. But when you find yourself looking down a gun barrel or lying with your face on the floor mat of Russo's shiny new Cadillac, don't forget there's one little flaw in your M.O. that we haven't even discussed yet."

"What's that?"

"It's your unfortunate habit of wandering around like a kid playing blindman's buff. You've admitted to me, several times, that you just 'follow your nose,' as you put it, until—surprise—there you are: you've found your murderer. You can reach out and touch him—and he can touch you. With whatever's handy. So far, you've been lucky. All your murderers've been amateurs, just like you. Either that, or the police haven't been far behind. But you can't buck the odds in this business, Steve. For a while you can, but sooner or later you come a cropper. Ninety-five times out of a hundred, we could run things with just one man in a squad car, for instance. We could do the job a lot cheaper, and make the taxpayers a lot happier. But then comes the ninety-sixth time. And it means a man's life. It's as simple as that."

"Well, I think you're exaggerating. You—"

"All right," he interrupted sharply, raising a peremptory hand. "If you won't listen to anything else I've said, for God's sake, remember this: whatever you do, have the basic, elementary common sense not to stay in La Palada. Not that it'll make a damn bit of difference, if they decide to—to discipline you. But at least you'll be in more or less friendly territory."

"All right, that's good advice. How far is La Palada from Los Angeles?"

"Just a few miles, depending on where you are in

30

L.A.," he answered moodily. "As a matter of fact, I know of a good place for you to stay. It's the Prescott Motel. It's a nice place, and it's not far from La Palada. Not too expensive either."

"Good. Thanks. Do you think I should notify the CIIB before I go? As a precaution?"

"Oh, for . . ." He slammed down his cup, hard. His voice was loud and exasperated as he said, "Can't you get it through your head what you're getting yourself into? If you notify the CIIB, the first thing they'll do is put a tail on you. Either that, or they'll demand that you inform for them. But either way, you'd be cutting your chances of survival by about three hundred per cent. It's bad enough, your wandering down to see Russo like he was some—some potentate in the Shriners, or something. But for God's sake, keep your—your innocence. It's the only thing that'll get you back in one piece. It's bad enough, you're coming here. That was stupid enough, if you really want my opinion. But if you go to the CIIB, or the FBI, you're just asking for—"

Suddenly the kitchen door opened. Mrs. Larsen entered, smiling.

"You're raising your voice, George," she observed, cheerfully. "Did Steve do something else to make your detectives look silly?"

He stared at her and snorted.

"Not this time, Carrie," he said. "Not this time."

3

By the time I'd rented a car, drove across Los Angeles, and lost my way three times on the freeways before finally finding the Prescott Motel, it was after ten o'clock Saturday night. But Larsen had been right; the Prescott was a good motel, although not as reasonable as I'd hoped. I unpacked, changed into a sport coat and found my way to the dining room for a belated dinner. The motel was laid out in a wagon-wheel pattern, so that each room opened both on the outdoors and also on a hallway leading to the hub, containing the dining room, bar and lobby.

After dinner, out of curiosity, I asked for a La Palada phone book. First I looked up Frank Russo. There was a listing for "F. Russo," which seemed close enough. Next I tried Mrs. Vennezio. She, too, was listed, and I also found an F. Hanson, which might be Dominic Vennezio's mistress. Reflecting that I'd exhausted all the contacts I had in the Vennezio murder, I decided to have a drink and take stock. Since the time was almost eleven, I had no desire to call Mrs. Vennezio, and certainly I wasn't going to call Russo for an appointment—or, for that matter,

Mrs. Hanson.

Over the drink I began thinking about my conversation with Larsen, and in the darkness of the bar, surrounded by strangers, I suddenly experienced a very lost, very lonely feeling. Larsen had been right. I'd been a vain, shortsighted fool to accept Mrs. Vennezio's strange, illogical proposition. At best, I was a gifted amateur—with a gift that even I couldn't define. Only the week before I'd read in a popular magazine that a noted psychologist considered clairvoyance in humans to be essentially the same as instinct in the lower animals and therefore no more remarkable than, say, the migratory instinct in birds. The author had then concluded with the speculation that clairvoyants were perhaps lower down on the evolutionary scale than ordinary humans.

Larsen had also been right about the publicity I'd received. Most of it had been self-serving, cynically calculated to increase the *Sentinel's* circulation. True, on at least three occasions during the past few years I'd discovered a murderer. The first time had been an accident: the random flash of a wayward image on my unsuspecting consciousness, turning my footsteps blindly toward the spot where a murderer crouched in the darkness, gibbering. By chance's caprice, the story had been picked up by the wire services. I'd been working for a small San Jose daily, and within a week's time the *San Francisco Sentinel* had offered to double my salary and give me a by-line. Other successes had followed—and some failures. At first, the police were derisive, even hostile. But the police were always there. We were on the same side.

This was different. This time, I was on my own. I was in a strange town, staying in a strange motel, drinking in a strange, lonely bar.

As I paid for the drink and slipped off the bar stool, I was conscious that the phrase *Pride goeth before a fall* was beginning to revolve in my thoughts. It was a phrase my father had been fond of quoting. For him it had always had a special meaning. For me it had always been a pointless parental aphorism.

Larsen had put it another way, warning me not to become the victim of my own publicity. If the Bible were to be written in today's idiom, I was thinking as I walked down the long corridor to my room, that's the way a disciple might phrase it: don't believe your own publicity.

By ten the following morning I'd had breakfast and was standing in a telephone booth, staring at the name *F. Russo*, and the number, 824-4076.

Should I wait until tomorrow, Monday?

Should I give it up and get a plane back to San Francisco?

As a teen-ager, trying to get up the nerve to call a girl, I could remember standing in exactly the same uncertain posture and feeling the same sheepish doubts. I hadn't liked the feeling then, and I didn't like it now. It was only a phone call. I wasn't committing myself to anything. I'd come four hundred miles and I'd spend a hundred dollars before I got back to San Francisco. If I'd been a fool to take the job, I was being a bigger fool now—and a timid one, at that.

I was dialing the number; the line was ringing. Was it Frankie Russo's phone? F. Russo? It seemed incredible that—

"Hello?" It was a man's voice.

34

"Is this—" I cleared my throat. "Is this Mr. Russo? Frank Russo?"

"No. Mr. Russo can't come to the phone right now. Who's calling?" The voice was brusk, impatient.

"Well, this is—I'm Stephen Drake. I—"

"Is Mr. Russo expecting you to call him?"

"Well, I don't know. That is, I'm not sure. Mrs. Vennezio—Mrs. Dominic Vennezio—made an appointment for me with Mr. Russo. She said that I should—"

"Just a minute." The line clicked dead. I shifted the receiver from one ear to the other. As I did, I realized that the receiver was streaked with moisture. But at least now I was only a fool, no longer a timid one.

"Hello?" It was a different voice, heavier.

"Yes. Hello."

"This is Frank Russo. Are you the party that Aidia Vennezio went up to San Francisco to see Friday?"

"Y—yes, I am."

"What's your name again?"

"Drake. Stephen Drake. Mrs. Vennezio said that I should—"

"Where are you now, Mr. Drake?"

"I'm in Los Angeles. I . . . ." Desperately, I tried to decide whether I should give him the name of the motel. Larsen hadn't . . .

"Where, in Los Angeles?"

"Well, I'm not sure. I've only been in Los Angeles two or three times, and I—"

"What place is it, that you're staying?"

"It—it's the Prescott Motel. But I—"

"Just a minute." This time, the phone was covered. Then: "I'll send someone for you. His name is Montez.

35

Jimmy Montez. He should be there inside a half hour."

"But I've got a car. I could—"

"That's all right. This place is hard to find. I'll see you in about an hour." The line went dead.

As I replaced the receiver, I felt an unexpected sense of satisfaction—almost a smugness. Frankie Russo hadn't sounded much different from any other business executive. He was a little less polished than some perhaps, but the short, crisp phrases and the brisk, decisive manner had been the same.

It was, after all, a business—big business. Chicago in the thirties had been one thing. This was Los Angeles. Lotus Land, thirty years later.

I decided to have a second cup of coffee and then wait for Jimmy Montez in the lobby.

Montez moved with the lithe, elegant grace of a bull-fighter. He was wearing an expensive orange silk sport shirt, narrow-cut tan gabardine slacks and beautifully burnished brown loafers. His black hair curled down low on his bronze neck, and he walked with a long, light stride. His smile was wide and quick; his teeth were very white. His dark, restless eyes seemed both friendly and shrewd.

"Just down here," he said, as we left the motel lobby. "It's that Buick, there." He pointed to a beige sedan parked at the curb. Walking quickly a few paces ahead, he opened the passenger door for me, then briskly closed it. I watched him circle the car, whistling. His hand lingered on the gleaming hood, lightly caressing the metal.

The car smelled new. As we pulled away from the curb

I said, "Nice car."

He flashed me his quick, youthful smile. "We've only had it three weeks. It's not even broken in yet. Mr. Russo got two at the same time. Two Buicks. He gets a better deal, that way. He does it every year."

"Do you drive for Mr. Russo?"

Some of his good humor seemed to fade.

"Mostly that's what I do. But it's only been a year, since I started with him." His manner became defensive. "Mr. Russo likes people to start at the bottom."

I was thinking of the prohibition era gangsters, and of tommy guns blazing through the drawn side curtains of careening cars. In those days, a wheelman had status. Now it was the era of the crooked accountants and lawyers, with a talent for either hoodwinking or discreetly bribing their opposite numbers.

"What're you going to do for Mr. Russo?" he asked, looking at me with a cheerful derision. "Are you one of those college graduates he talks about?"

"Well, I . . ."

"I'll bet anything you're a college graduate. Aren't you?" His voice now had a certain insistent edge.

"Well, yes, I am, as a matter of fact."

He nodded, satisfied. "I knew it. I'm getting so I can tell. I don't mean just about being a college graduate, but about people. Mr. Russo says that's the most important thing, to be able to judge people. If you can do that, he says—judge people—you can figure out which way they'll jump. And when you can figure that, you've got it made. Because most people don't know themselves which way they'll jump. That's what Mr. Russo says. And he's right. I've seen it happen."

37

I decided not to reply, but instead looked out the window. We were entering the freeway. Montez held the car in a long, graceful curve, expertly. Obviously he enjoyed driving, as only a young man with expensive dreams can enjoy handling a big, powerful automobile.

"Not too far now," he said, his eyes on the road. "Eight, nine miles. No more."

"What did you do before you worked for Mr. Russo?" I asked.

He shrugged. "I was in and out of jail. I was a real nowhere kid. Tough, you know what I mean? Tough and dumb. The last time I did, it was for knifing some guy I'd never seen before in my life. And you know why? Because a girl just wanted to see us fight."

"How old were you?"

"Nineteen. And it cost me almost three years, that fight. And it was hard time, too. My juvenile record went against me, plus I stayed dumb on the inside. I still thought I had to be tough. Then, just about six months before I got out, I met this guy Danny Frichetti, who'd worked for Mr. Russo back in Kansas City. We were cellmates, Danny and me. He was older than me, but he liked me. He said I could get somewhere, if I'd only cool down and use my head. He told me to see Mr. Russo when I got out. Danny'd heard that Mr. Russo had just come out to the Coast."

"That was just about a year ago, then."

"Right. I first got a job in a dry cleaning plant, through parole. But I saw Mr. Russo, and he got me fixed up right away. I'm supposed to be working in a cigar store. Technically." He half-turned his head and smiled. "You know."

I nodded. Then, casually, I asked, "Did you always work for Mr. Russo? Or did you really work for Dominic Vennezio?"

He shot me a cautious glance. But the answer came readily enough.

"I guess you'd say that we all worked for Vennezio, until—a few weeks ago. But the only one I ever saw was Mr. Russo. Vennezio was someone I just heard about, and used to see once in a while. But I drove for Mr. Russo, right from the start. And did—other things. You know." Again he glanced at me, thought about it for a moment and then asked, "Are you from the East?"

"No. I'm from San Francisco. I just got in last night."

He nodded, but didn't reply. The car was slowing, and ahead I saw a sign marking the La Palada freeway exit. Briefly I considered more leading questions, but then decided against it. Montez would willingly talk about himself, but my first mention of Vennezio had brought a wary question in return. Until Montez knew more of my credentials, he would tell me nothing.

So, instead, I asked, "Have you lived in Los Angeles all your life?"

I saw his eyes flicker in a spasm of opaque bitterness.

"That's right. All my life. Some life." He pointed up ahead. "Here we are."

We'd been traveling on a narrow concrete road, and now we turned off on a graveled road marked "Private." The road climbed for perhaps a quarter-mile, through a grove of eucalyptus trees. Then, suddenly, we were pulling into a parking area topped with crushed rock, gleaming sparkling white in the warm September sunshine. The car came to a stop before a long, low, three-car garage. I got out, aware that my first reaction was a sense of relief. Unconsciously, perhaps, I'd been expecting a tall, foreboding fortress of a house surrounded by a high cyclone fence, guarded by vicious dogs and electric eyes. Instead, I saw the shake roofs and the expansive redwood-and-glass architecture of California's upper middle class.

"We can go through here," Montez said, leading the way down a graveled path and through a gate set into a grape stake fence. "Mr. Russo's out by the pool. He said you should come out there."

The pool, like the house and grounds, was more than merely adequate, but not ostentatious. Two men, both wearing bathing trunks, sat together in the shade of a small cabana. Both men were heavy-set and deeply tanned. One man, balding, wore heavy black-rimmed glasses; the other had thick, wiry gray hair, carefully groomed and trimmed. Both seemed common poolside types, paunchy and prosperous, relaxing in the sun.

As we approached, neither rose. The balding man gestured to a nearby metal chair, which Montez pulled up for me.

"Mr. Drake?" the balding man asked.

"Yes," I answered, still standing.

"I'm Frank Russo. This is Martin Franklin. Sit down."

"Thank you." I sat facing the two men. As I did, I realized that Montez, without speaking, had already disappeared. And now Martin Franklin got to his feet. He paused to drain the last of a tall drink, then said to Russo, "I'll have everything ready for you to sign by tomorrow afternoon, Frank. Shall I send the papers over to the office, or here?"

"Send them to the office. If I'm not there, Gloria'll

know where I am. She'll get them to me."

"Good. Why don't you bring them home with you tomorrow evening? I'll pick them up after work."

"All right. Fine."

"I'd better be going." Franklin glanced at his watch. "It's almost noon."

"See you tomorrow."

"Right." Franklin nodded to me, smiled automatically and began walking across the lawn toward the house. As I turned my gaze to Russo, I realized that he'd been studying me. His dark, quick eyes were small and intent behind his heavy glasses. His face, even with a Sunday's growth of beard, had the smooth, bland, well-barbered look of the successful, fortyish businessman. The relaxed lines of his body, reclining in a cord-and-metal lounge chair, projected a semi-indolent aura of affluence and command, comfortably assured. His face was broad and swarthy, his jowls were beginning to sag. His torso, thickening, was still well-muscled. In his twenties, I decided, Frank Russo must have been a powerfully built young man.

Now he gestured to a nearby table full of bottles, glasses and an ice bucket.

"Drink?"

"No, thanks."

"Usually I never drink before five o'clock. Never. On Sundays, though, it's different." As if to make the point, he sipped from the glass at his side, then once more resumed his open appraisal of me.

"You look different than I'd figured," he said finally. "You look just like anyone. Anyone at all."

Something about the candid, almost ingenuous blunt-

41

ness of the remark made me smile, involuntarily.

"That's the way I feel," I answered. "Just like anyone else."

He nodded thoughtfully. Slowly he put the highball aside, with the air of a man whose thoughts were half-regretfully turning to business instead of to swimming or sunbathing.

"I hear you're a crime reporter up in San Francisco."

"That's right." I tried to keep my eyes steady as I met his narrow, dark gaze.

"I also hear," he continued, "that you're one of these guys who can figure out where the body's buried just by closing your eyes and getting a picture about it." He paused, obviously waiting for a reply.

"That's right, too." I decided not to elaborate. As long as he was asking the questions, I was content to answer, hopefully in a firm, quiet voice.

"As far as I'm concerned," he said bluntly, "that stuff's all a bunch of crap."

I shrugged. "I know just how you feel. A few years ago, I'd've said the same thing myself."

He nodded, chewing reflectively at his lower lip. "That's not a bad answer. I guess I'd say the same thing myself, if I was you."

I didn't reply. Over the past few years I'd watched many people try, in many different ways, to bait me on the subject of clairvoyance. My best defense, I'd learned, was complete honesty.

"Aidia Vennezio is a religious nut," he said abruptly. "She's superstitious. She doesn't know what she's doing."

"She wants to find out who murdered her husband. That's what she told me."

"Did you tell her that you'd do it?" Now there was a certain watchful stillness in his manner.

"I said I'd come down and talk to you."

"Did she pay you for coming?"

I nodded. "She paid me a thousand dollars." I'd already decided to tell him, because I was sure he must know.

Now he smiled, apparently in genuine good humor. His mouth was full and wide, and the expression was almost a pleasant one.

"You're honest, anyhow. It's hard to find an honest man these days."

"I know. I feel the same way."

"What'll you do if I don't like the idea of you nosing around?"

"I'll go back to San Francisco."

"Did you tell Aidia that?"

"I'm not sure whether I did or not, in so many words. But that was the understanding. I can go back to San Francisco any time I like."

"And you'll be a thousand dollars richer."

"Yes."

"Well, that's not bad dough. A thousand dollars a day. I could live on that."

"It doesn't come along often, though."

He reached for his highball, then raised the glass to me. "Sure you won't have one?"

"No, thanks."

For a long moment he sipped the drink, watching me. Then, putting the glass aside, he sat up straighter. His manner became crisper as he said, "What d'you write about, exactly, when you report on crime?"

I thought for a moment before saying, "Mostly, I

43

suppose, it's murders. That's what the people like to read about. So that's what we write."

"Ever write much on gambling?"

"Not much. Most people gamble, one way or the other. So they don't enjoy reading about it. It's not news."

"Are there many bookie operations going in San Francisco?"

"Yes," I answered, as steadily as I could. "San Francisco's no different than any other city. There's always a place to put down a bet."

"Do you ever write anything about that?"

"No, I never have."

"What about cops? Don't you write about how they should close down the books?"

I sighed. I thought I could see where the conversation was going. I didn't like it, but I'd passed the point of squeamish scruples the day before. It seemed very long ago.

"We get our news from the police," I said. "You can't bite the hand that feeds you."

"Have you ever heard of cops up in San Francisco taking payoffs?"

"Yes, I've heard of it. I've been on the crime beat for five years. I've heard a lot of things."

"Have you heard about me?"

I realized I was gripping the arms of my chair. With a conscious effort I relaxed my hands, then settled back.

"Yes, I've heard about you."

"What've you heard?"

"I heard that you took over Dominic Vennezio's job."

He nodded, almost benignly.

"What else did you hear?"

44

I felt the barb of a quick impatience. I'd never liked being quizzed. I didn't like it now.

"I'm a reporter," I said. "I've heard a lot of things about you. Some of it I believe, some of it I don't. I know that Dominic Vennezio had the reputation for being the head of the Outfit down here. If you've taken his job, then I imagine that's what you're doing. But I don't really much care, if you want the truth. I'm not making any judgments. I'm a reporter, not a cop. I'll admit that I wanted to talk to you—very much. You're news, and that's—"

"What'd Aidia say about how Dom got killed?" he interrupted.

"She doesn't know who did it. And she doesn't think you do, either," I answered promptly. I realized that, surprisingly, I'd taken courage from my own waspish monologue.

"Do you believe her?"

"How should I know?" I was aware that my voice had slipped to a plaintive note. I wished he'd go for his Sunday swim and let me go back to San Francisco.

"How about this ESP?" he was asking. "How's it done? I mean, do you go into a trance, or what?"

"No, I don't go into a trance. It's difficult to explain in a few words, but basically it's a simple matter of being in contact with your own subconscious. Or, at least, that's what the experts say. As far as I'm concerned, I just—just wait for it to happen. And hope. It's a very unpredictable thing, believe me."

"I read an article about you two or three years ago, in *Newsweek*." He seemed to stress the title. "I was interested. I really was. I remember they said something

45

about the subconscious, too, like you say. They said it was like an iceberg. The 90 per cent that's under the water, that's the subconscious. The other part is the way we think, just about anything." He paused, frowning. Then, unexpectedly, he asked, "Did you go to college?"

"Yes. I studied jounalism."

"That fella that was just here . . ." He pointed to the empty chair. "He's my lawyer."

"I gathered that."

He nodded, staring at me with eyes narrowed and jaw thrust forward. I was remembering the remark Montez had made about the college graduates Russo employed.

I realized that I was beginning to squirm. And then, surprisingly, I realized that I wasn't squirming from fear or nervousness, but rather from irritation and impatience. Russo, in the flesh, didn't intimidate me. He was just another forceful, aggressive, self-made man who couldn't manage his syntax as well as he managed his bank balance.

"You know," he said suddenly, his voice a little louder. "You know, I like you. You're all right. The trouble with my business, you never have a chance to meet guys with any real class. Everyone's either yessing you or else they're out to get you. And you get tired of it. I been on my own since I was twenty years old. And I've done all right, too. But all my life I haven't had anything but third-rate guys around me. Tough guys. That's all they think about, how tough they are. You know what I mean?"

"Yes, I know what you mean."

"Like Dominic. He was a tough guy. And look what it got him. Dead."

46

I decided not to answer. If he was ready to talk, I was ready to listen.

"You know what I've got a good mind to do?" he said, leaning forward. "I've got a good mind to let you go ahead and see what you can find out. I'd like to see what happens." Then, frowning, he added, "If you didn't do this other—this crime reporting—you wouldn't even be here, believe me. But when I heard about it, I figured you must be a guy who knows how things are. Right?"

I felt myself nodding. I knew how things were. Larsen knew, too.

"What I mean is," he continued, his voice lowering to a more purposeful, more confidential note, "I've talked with a few reporters in my time. And I've talked to a few cops, too. I guess I don't have to tell you that. And it's like you said a little while ago, you've got to live and let live. But if someone gets out of line, no matter which side he's on, he gets his knuckles rapped. Right?"

I cleared my throat. "Yes. Right."

For a long, intent moment he stared directly into my eyes, still sitting hunched forward in his chair.

"What I mean," he said, "is that I don't want you talking to anyone, without you first talk to me. That means Aidia, or the cops or anyone else. If you get a—a picture, you tell it to me first. Right?"

I nodded, slowly.

He raised his hand and deliberately pointed his index finger directly at my forehead. As he did, he closed one eye, sighting along the finger.

"You're sure you understand me, now? You're a nice young guy. I like you, like I said. You've got class. So I wouldn't want there to be any misunderstanding." He

47

lowered his forefinger, still staring at me with his small dark eyes. "You understand?"

All I could think about was Larsen's similar gesture: the long forefinger, pointing in warning.

"Yes," I answered. "Yes, I understand."

Immediately he smiled, settling back in his chair.

"Good." He said it loudly, heartily. Then, reaching to the bottle-laden table, he said, "Now we'll drink. What'll you have?"

"Well, I'll—I'll have a vodka and tonic, if you've got it."

"Perfect. That's what I'm drinking." Rapidly he filled the glasses and handed mine over.

"Now," he said briskly, "how're you going to tackle this? Give me the rundown."

"Well, I'm not sure. I have to get all the information I can about Dominic Vennezio. Then I have to—to just start looking around until I find something. If I'm lucky, I get a feeling that it's something special. But . . ." I broke off, and gulped down a third of my drink. My hand was unsteady, but the glass didn't shake.

"Well, you won't get much from Aidia," he said decisively. "I can tell you that. All she can think about is how Dom took up with another woman. That's all she's got on her mind. That and Dom's murder."

"What can you tell me, Mr. Russo?"

"Call me Frank. What'd they call you? Steve?"

"Yes. Steve."

"Good. Well, there's not much I can tell you that'd mean anything. I mean, Dom had his troubles, like the rest of us, but it wasn't anything serious."

"What kind of troubles?"

He thought about it a moment before saying carefully, "Maybe Aidia told you some of it. Frank always liked the girls. That's all right. All of us do. But when he got hooked on this Hanson woman, things started to slide a little. He didn't pay attention to business, like he should. That's when I came out to the Coast, about a year ago." He paused. Then, choosing his words, he said, "Some of the newspapers figured that the two went together: me coming out, and Dom getting killed. But you know as well as I do, it doesn't happen like that anymore. Sure, Dom didn't have the zip he used to have. And, sure, I was running things, mostly, for the past six months or so. But Dom, he didn't really care. He had his. He had more real estate than you have ribbons for your typewriter. There wasn't any beef; he would've retired. It was all worked out, as a matter of fact. Another year, and he'd've been out to pasture, playing with his girl friend."

"Then you must've been disturbed by his murder."

"You're damn right I was. I can tell you, things were pretty rough around here."

"How do you mean?"

"Well, no one knew where they stood. They were nervous. I mean, they didn't know what to think. Especially the way Dom was killed. It was like—well, it was like the old days."

"How do you mean?"

"I mean, it was a clean job. It looked like a professional job. It still does." He said it almost indignantly. "That's what I say, everyone got nervous. Even the cops. Maybe you know that we've got things pretty well under control here in La Palada. I mean, we've got the lowest crime rate in the state. So when this thing blew up, everyone got hot as hell. I even had to go back East and explain things. As a matter of fact . . ." He smiled to himself, in covert satisfaction. "As a matter of fact, when Aidia came to me, all wide-eyed, and said she was going to hire you, I first of all let her think I didn't like it. Maybe at first I didn't. But then, when I'd had a chance to think about it, I told her to go ahead, provided you talked to me first. I was even thinking of hiring a private detective to look into things for me. I didn't do it, but I was thinking about it. So now . . ." He waved his glass at me. "Now Aidia's spending her money. And just as long as we all understand each other, nobody'll get burned."

"What would happen if I should discover that the murderer was actually an—associate of yours?"

"That'd depend on who it was and why he did it. But that'd be my business." He looked at me meaningfully. "It doesn't have anything to do with you. Right?"

I nodded. I was feeling a little more irked each time he stared at me with his bully's black eyes and said "Right?" I finished my drink, anxious to be gone.

"You don't really have any idea who did it, then?" I asked.

He spread his hands. "None at all. I'm as much in the dark as Aidia, except that I'm not as bugged. Everything's settled down, and Dom was dead weight anyhow. There's no sweat. I'd still like to know who did it, but I'm not hurting." He drained his own drink, glanced at his watch and heaved himself to his feet. As I also stood, he looked me up and down, smiling.

"You know," he said, clapping me heavily on the shoulder and turning me toward the grape stake fence. "You know, you don't look to me like a real rugged guy. You'd

50

better take care of yourself. Don't take any chances, and stay loose. If you need anything, let me know. Call me anytime. I have someone that answers the phone, most of the time. I'll give him the word. He'll know where to find me, and he'll put you right through."

"All right, I will."

"Good." We'd reached the gate, which my host opened. Montez was standing by the Buick, waiting. Russo extended his hand.

"Good luck, Steve," he said smiling. Then, allowing the smile to fade, he said, "And be sure and remember what I said. *Everything* I said."

"Thanks, Frank. I will."

"Good." He nodded, unsmiling now. Then he turned back to the pool, closing the gate behind him.

4

I'D HALF-EXPECTED Faith Hanson to put me off, but when I called her later Sunday afternoon she seemed almost anxious to talk with me. She spent several minutes giving me detailed driving directions, and with the aid of a La Palada Chamber of Commerce map I easily found her house.

It was a modest stucco bungalow, California-ersatz-Spanish, with an imitation-tile roof and matching red tile entryway. Three spiky palms dominated the small, neatly mowed front lawn, and a flagstone sidewalk led to an ornately paneled front door.

As I rang the bell I tried to picture her, finally deciding on the image of a medium-sized brunette, full-figured and heavily made up, wearing capri stretch pants and a pastel-colored bulky-knit sweater.

The image was wrong. She was rather small, almost petite. Her ash-blond hair was simply worn, and her heather-hued dress was conservatively cut. Her wide-set gray eyes were calm and appraising.

We introduced ourselves, and she showed me into her small living room. The furniture was richly carved in the

Mediterranean style; the polished floors were covered with a colorful collection of small oriental rugs.

As we sat in facing easy chairs, I decided that Mrs. Hanson possessed taste, composure and probably intelligence. The restrained, graceful economy of her movements suggested a kind of elegant, understated sensuality—something special for a special man, but not for public display.

"Would you like a drink?" she asked.

"No, thanks. I, ah, won't stay very long, Mrs. Hanson. I just wanted to ask you a few questions." I drew a deep breath, deciding to come directly to the point.

"As I told you on the phone, I've been retained to look into the death of Dominic Vennezio. I've talked to Mrs. Vennezio, and I've talked to Frank Russo. Now, if it's all right, I'd like to talk to you."

"You didn't say who retained you." As she spoke, she held herself rigidly—back arched, knees tight together. Her voice had a low, breathless quality. She was obviously exercising a painful, precarious self-control.

"Mrs. Vennezio retained me," I answered, content for the moment merely to watch her. Against what emotion was she bracing herself so rigidly? Was it grief? Fear? Guilt? If fear or guilt were her problem, why had she so willingly agreed to see me?

"Mrs. Vennezio," she repeated, her voice expressionless. Her eyes were fixed unblinkingly on my own, yet I felt that only an enormous effort of will kept her eyes so steady. She seemed somehow strangely compelled to respond to my questions, almost as if she were speaking from the depths of a hypnotist's trance.

"Yes," I answered. "Even though they were separated,

53

Mrs. Vennezio is naturally anxious to know who murdered her husband. I'm sure you can understand that."

She nodded, woodenly. Then she asked, "Are you a private detective, Mr. Drake?"

I somehow felt unwilling to become enmeshed in the lengthy business of explaining my alleged prowess of clairvoyance. So I simply nodded. She seemed to accept it. Immediately, I wondered whether she thought I'd come representing the Outfit. It would be a possible explanation for her curiously hushed responses. Fear paralyzed, especially if guilt were the catalyst.

Perhaps I had my opening.

Lowering my voice to a more impersonal note, I said, "Would you mind telling me something of your relationship with Dominic Vennezio, Mrs. Hanson?" Then, thinking about it, I hastily amended: "That is, when did you meet him, how often did you see him, et cetera?"

"I've known him—" She blinked and swallowed. "I knew him for about two years." Her voice was still controlled, her eyes were still steady. But her fingers, I noticed, incessently twisted. Her legs, I also noticed, were beautifully shaped.

"You were working in a real estate office, I understand, when you first met him."

"Yes."

"And then, soon afterward, Mr. Vennezio set up his own real estate office. And you worked for him. Is that right?"

She nodded. Waiting. Again I felt the resignation with which she answered me—and the strange compulsion.

"And you became, ah, friends."

For a moment she remained perfectly motionless, star-

54

ing at me with her wide-set gray eyes. Then, very distinctly, she said:

"I became his mistress."

I drew a deep breath. I was infuriatingly aware that I must be blushing as I said, "Thank you for being so honest, Mrs. Hanson. It's very helpful."

With a quiet, ironic sarcasm she said, "Do I have a choice?"

"How do you mean?"

"I mean that I've been waiting for you—or someone like you—ever since they killed Dominic. I'm only surprised that it took so long. And I'm also surprised at you."

"At me?" I felt myself suddenly at a sheepish loss.

She nodded. "You're much different from what I'd expected. I've only met a few of Dom's—associates—but none of them was like you."

"But I'm not—I mean—" I realized that I was shifting uncomfortably in my chair, squirming before her increasingly obvious scorn.

"I know. You don't work for them. Not really. I wasn't a gangster's girl friend, either. Not really. That's what the other women were. I was something special. I have 'class,' as Dominic used to say. Refinement."

Suddenly I felt a sense of shame. Should I try to explain? I decided against it. She could be answering out of fear, feeling that she only had a choice between my questions or something much worse. If I disassociated myself from the Outfit, therefore, I might be the loser.

And, besides, she was right. Since noon that day, I'd been an employee of the Outfit—or at least a tacit associate.

So, with a kind of hostile guilt I took the role of the impersonal inquisitor.

"Tell me something about your life before you met Dominic, Mrs. Hanson."

"What would you like to know? How far back should I start?"

I shrugged. I was aware of a rising cynicism in myself—a blunt, bitter response to her own cynical, self-debasing hostility.

"Start wherever you like."

Silently she looked at me, deciding. In her tightened mouth and chilled gray eyes I could plainly see contempt. Then, with a slow, eloquent movement she raised her shoulders, seemingly indifferent. She began speaking in a low, precise monotone. Her voice seemed to express both the numbness of defeat and the defiance of someone with no more to lose.

"It all started, I suppose, forty-one years ago, when I was born. That's where it always starts, I'm told. My father was an awning salesman—a successful awning salesman. He made a good living. However, unfortunately, he always spent more than he made. My mother, you see, appreciated the finer things in life. Her family, we were always told, had raised her to expect the best and to act accordingly. So we were always in debt. Then, when the depression came, my father lost everything. He got some of it back, of course, during the war, but he was never quite the same. Neither was my mother. She never let him forget that he'd failed. Never. So, gradually, my father became a—a hollow man. And my mother became bitter. Brittle, and bitter."

I sighed. "That's a common story."

She smiled with a kind of pensive, wistful regret. "The rest is common enough, too. During my last year in college my parents finally got divorced, so when I graduated I decided to come out to California, to San Francisco. I had an aunt in San Francisco, my mother's sister. She got me a suitable job, in the financial district, and found me the right kind of apartment, in the right neighborhood. And, in due time, I met the right kind of a young man. John Hanson. We got married, after a glittering kind of cocktail-party courtship. And then, slowly, I proceeded to do to my husband what my mother had done to my father."

"How . . ." I cleared my throat. "How do you mean?"

"John was a stockbroker," she said softly. "A young, bright, golden-haired stockbroker, with a wonderful smile and a boyish charm. His family was well off and even had social pretensions. They could afford to go to the opera and to charity balls, and once in a while they got their names in the society columns. And so did John and I, occasionally. We were a handsome young couple, you see, and we lived on Russian Hill and drove a sportscar and sailed and had a Japanese couple cater when we gave cocktail parties. That was in 1948 and 1949. We were both happy, I suppose. But then, unfortunately, it became increasingly apparent that John wasn't really a very good stockbroker. He was good at entertaining people, especially in bars, but he wasn't good at selling them stocks or bonds. So John's parents started giving us money, 'until we got on our feet.' And the more money they gave us, the less John worked. And the more he drank."

"That's a common story, too"

She nodded. "So is the last of it, too, I suppose. I decided that what we needed was a child, to bring us closer together and give John a sense of responsibility. Unfortunately, however, the child was conceived at almost exactly the time North Korea invaded South Korea—and John was in the reserve."

She sighed. "In a way, Korea was John's last chance. He was a pilot, flying cargo planes, and he liked it. When his Korean tour was over, he told me that he wanted to stay in the Air Force. But I wouldn't let him. My mother, I suppose, had told me it was a ghastly life, being an army wife. So, anyhow, John went back with his old company, selling stocks. Except that, this time, he didn't even make any pretense of working. He just stayed in the bars all day and drank. Sometimes he'd go to movies, and once a week or so he'd visit an old girl friend who'd just got divorced. He was never obvious about it, though, or inconsiderate. John was always considerate and really very sweet. He would have made a good husband, probably, if he'd stayed in the Air Force. The army can be a good place for weaklings."

"What happened then, Mrs. Hanson?"

"Well finally, after a year or so, John became an embarrassment to his family—and to me. So we decided, his family and I, that the best thing for John would be for us to move to Los Angeles. If we could get John away from his old environment, we decided, everything would be all right. And also, as part of the therapy, John's family would stop sending us money. As it turned out, there was more than just therapy involved. Mr. Hanson's business was failing, and two years later, in the recession of 1958, it failed altogether. By that time, of course, we'd come to

Los Angeles. John was selling 'real estate,' instead of 'selling stocks.'" Bitterly she accented the two phrases. "And instead of his parents giving us money 'until we got on our feet,' I began working. Full time. I became very good at real estate escrow. And, over the years, I had various affairs with various men. Somehow it was the only thing left."

"You and John had a child, did you say?"

A brief spasm twitched at her face.

"Yes, Mr. Drake. We had a child. John Hanson the third. He was a beautiful boy. He still is a beautiful boy, only now he's sixteen. He doesn't need me anymore. He never did, really. That was my husband's single virtue, you see: he loved his son. He loved Johnny, and he understood him. I suppose, in many ways, John was really more a boy than a man. He was defenseless, and innocent, and . . ." She swallowed, then continued in a firmer voice:

"When I had to go to work, my husband looked after Johnny. He'd even pace himself, drinking, to fit Johnny's schedule." She paused, staring down at her hands. "I've often wondered whether that's why I started with other men—because my husband, for all his faults and his weakness, really meant more to Johnny than I did. I don't know. I do know, though, that men became more and more important to me. Wealthy, aggressive men. Men with drive and ambition."

"And that's how you met Dominic Vennezio."

She raised her head in the timeless gesture of the fallen woman, defiant in her fall.

"Yes, Mr. Drake. That's how I met Dominic."

"And . . ." I hesitated. "What happened to your hus-

59

band, Mrs. Hanson, after you met Vennezio?"

"Shortly after I met Dominic, and began—seeing him, John left."

"Do you know where he went?"

"I understand he went back to San Francisco."

"Have you heard from him?"

"Not directly."

"But you know he's alive:"

"I've heard he's alive. I don't know for sure. He has a younger brother living here in Los Angeles. Bruce. If anything had happened to John and Bruce knew about it, I suppose I'd've heard."

I nodded, thinking about it. Finally, I said, "What about the boy? I mean, weren't you surprised that your husband would've left his son if they were so close?"

"Johnny was fourteen by then. They weren't close any longer."

"Is he—" Involuntarily I looked around. "Is the boy living with you?"

"He was, until this last year. Now he's going to Midfield. It's a boarding school in the Ojai Valley, just forty miles from Los Angeles."

"I see. And how long has it been since your husband left?"

She thought about it, then said, "Just about two years. I'd been working for Dominic three months, when John left."

"Were you living here at the time?"

She laughed with brief, bitter humor. "We were living in a one-room apartment. Drinking is an expensive habit, Mr. Drake, especially when there's only one income."

"Then . . ." I hesitated. "Then, if I understand the sequence correctly, first you met Dominic. Then, three months later, your husband moved out. And then, shortly afterward, you moved into this house. Is that right?"

She nodded. Her earlier defiance had gone—dissolved, perhaps, in a wayward moment of disillusioned, self-pitying introspection.

"Did Dominic ever tell you much about his business, Mrs. Hanson?"

"Never. At least, nothing about anything beyond real estate. Dominic had a passion for real estate. He owns—owned—several buildings in town. And he speculated in land, too."

"But he never mentioned the Outfit."

"No. Never."

"Were you aware that he was connected with organized crime?"

"Yes, of course. I read the papers, Mr. Drake."

"And did you realize that his, ah, affair with you might have caused him trouble?"

"Dominic was used to trouble. That was his business."

I hesitated. Then, abruptly, I asked, "Do you have any idea why he was killed, Mrs. Hanson?"

She raised her eyes to mine, looked at me for a long, silent moment and then shook her head.

"I've no idea. Beyond what I read in the papers."

"How did it actually happen, that you were the one to discover him?"

Her answer came almost too quickly, as if she'd been prepared for the question—almost as if her answer might have been overrehearsed.

"I always met Dominic at the beachhouse Sunday nights, when Johnny was visiting me. Johnny would usually leave about six thirty, for school. As soon as he'd left I'd change my clothes and pack a bag and then drive out to the beachhouse."

"Does your son have his own car?"

"Yes. He—Dom had just bought it for him. A Mustang."

"Does your son spend every weekend with you?"

"No. He—" She bit her lip. "He usually visits me every second or third weekend."

"Is he here this weekend?"

"Yes."

"Was he visiting you three weeks ago? When Dominic was killed?"

"Yes."

I nodded. "What time did you actually get to the beachhouse, Mrs. Hanson?"

"It was quarter after eight. Maybe a little later."

"What time did you leave here?"

"About seven thirty. It's a forty-five-minute drive on Sunday nights."

"And what did you find at the beachhouse? From the outside, was there anything unusual?"

She shook her head. "Nothing. I parked the car in the carport and took my suitcase and walked around to the front door, just as I always did. It wasn't until then that I realized anything was wrong."

"How do you mean?"

"The door was standing open."

"I see. What happened then?"

"Well, I—I just went inside. And . . ." She blinked. Her hands, I noticed, were once more twisting in her lap. Her body was rigid, and her chin was tilted painfully

62

upward.

"And then I saw him," she finished. "He was lying in the center of the living room. He was . . ." Again she blinked, rapidly. "He was staring up at the ceiling. Dead."

"Did the police say how long he'd been dead when you found him?"

"Less than an hour, they said."

"He'd been shot, is that right?"

"Yes. In the—the chest. Three times."

"Did all of the bullets strike him? I mean, did the police find any bullets that missed—went wild?"

"I—I don't know. I don't think so."

"Did any of the neighbors hear shots?"

"I don't know."

"Have you any idea who called the police?"

"No. I don't think the police know, either."

"Did Dominic mention any enemies?"

"No. Never."

"Did he seem worried, just before he was murdered?"

"No. In fact, he'd closed a deal the day before that netted him almost forty thousand dollars. We were going to drive to Malibu that night and celebrate."

"And you don't have any idea who might've killed him?"

She shook her head. "No, Mr. Drake, I don't." She was more relaxed now. She'd told her story. Obviously, she had nothing more to tell. And, just as obviously, she was telling the truth, with nothing to hide. She saw herself and her life with a painful clarity—just as she saw Dominic and their affair with the same uncompromising clarity, almost masochistically. Watching her simply sit star-

63

ing at me, waiting for my next questions, I wondered whether Faith Hanson might enjoy suffering. I wondered how many of her wealthy, successful, aggressive men may have mistreated her, either emotionally or physically.

I decided to put the theory to the test.

"Did Dominic ever mention his family to you, Mrs. Hanson?"

Momentarily she closed her eyes, as if braced for a blow. But her answer was steady.

"Yes, he did. Several times."

"Did he ever tell you that, when his wife moved out, she put away certain letters that might have sent Dominic to prison?"

She shook her head. "No, he never told me that."

"But he did talk to you about his wife."

"Yes."

"And he had two children, didn't he?"

"Yes."

"Did he ever talk about them?"

"He talked about his girl, Charlene. Often."

"Was he fond of her, would you say?"

"Yes, he was. They fought a lot, probably because they were so similar. But he loved her. It was obvious."

"Did she love him?"

She shrugged. "If you'll define 'love' for me, Mr. Drake, I'll answer the question."

I smiled. "I withdrew the question. How old is Charlene?"

"Twenty-six, I believe." She thought about it, then nodded. "Yes, she's twenty-six."

"Does she live here?"

64

"She lives in Los Angeles."

"Is she married?"

Momentarily she hesitated before shaking her head.

"Is she a pretty girl?"

"Yes. Very."

"Then why isn't she married, I wonder."

Again came the intriguing hesitation. Finally she said, cautiously, "I wouldn't know."

"I think you do, Mrs. Hanson."

She looked at me, then sighed. "Charlene is going around with one of Dominic's associates. That's the only thing he ever told me about his—his other business, when he mentioned Larry Sabella in relation to Charlene. Apparently Dominic had forbidden her to have anything to do with Sabella—or with any of those—men."

"But she defied her father. Is that it?"

"Yes."

"Is Sabella married, do you know?"

"I don't know. I don't believe so. That would've been the last straw, as far as Dominic was concerned."

"I see." I decided to shift my ground. "Is Dominic's other child a son?"

"Yes."

"How old is he?"

"Angelo is thirty, I think. Maybe thirty-one. He lives in Phoenix."

"What does he do, in Phoenix?"

"I'm not sure. But I gathered that he might be in the —the same line of work that Dominic was in."

"He works for the Outfit, you mean?"

She shrugged. She would say no more.

"Did he get along well with his father?"

65

Slowly she shook her head. "No, I don't believe they got along very well together. I think—I'm sure, really—that Dominic wanted Angelo to go into some—other line of work."

"But he didn't."

"No."

"Was Angelo capable, would you say? Intelligent?"

"I've never met Angelo," she answered. "But I'd say, offhand, that he probably isn't as intelligent as Charlene. Nor as—as fiery. I gather that Angelo is a lot more sullen than his sister. Both of them were problem children as teen-agers. But, of the two, Dominic always thought Charlene was high-spirited. Angelo, apparently, was just mean. He's even been in prison if I'm not mistaken. For manslaughter. Or at least he was indicted. Dominic never liked to talk about it."

"What kind of person was Dominic Vennezio, Mrs. Hanson?"

She looked at me, surprised.

"Didn't you know him?"

"I'd like to hear you describe him."

She looked at me speculatively. I wondered whether she might be considering some questions of her own. But finally she said, "Dominic was a simple, straightforward man. As long as you didn't antagonize him, he was just like anyone else. But, once he was crossed, he was a devil. If anyone lied to him or tried to get the best of him, fairly or unfairly, Dominic would do anything to get even. That's the way he operated in real estate, and I'm sure that in his—other business, he was even more ruthless."

"Was he intelligent, would you say?"

66

"He was intelligent enough. He had a good instinct for which people he could trust. And he was very shrewd. It took him a long time to figure out something, but when he finally made a decision it was usually right. And, too, he had a tremendous vitality. When he decided to enjoy himself, he went all the way. He was a high liver and a big spender. He wasn't ostentatious about it, especially, but he loved the feeling of being able to buy almost anything he wanted. And he did. I remember one time we were in a grocery store, and some children were buying candy. Dominic watched them. One boy bought five sticks of black licorice and left the store. Dominic went over to the candy counter and bought two whole boxes of black licorice. When I asked him why, he couldn't explain it, except to say that he remembered, as a kid, the thing he'd wanted more than anything else in the whole world was enough money to buy all the black licorice he wanted."

"Did he eat it?"

She smiled, her first expression of a genuine humor. "He ate a lot of it. And I helped him. I always liked licorice myself."

I answered her smile, then said, "If you had to guess, Mrs. Hanson, who would you say killed him?"

"I have no idea, Mr. Drake. There was a lot in Dominic's life that I didn't know anything about. I'm sure the police think someone in organized crime killed him. Don't you?"

"I don't know. And I don't think anyone else does, either. Did it ever occur to you, though, that you might've been killed yourself, if you'd arrived at the beachhouse maybe a half hour earlier?"

67

"Yes, I've thought about that. Often."

"Does the thought frighten you?"

"No, Mr. Drake, it doesn't. When I was a lot younger, and a lot happier, the thought of death used to terrify me. But now . . ." She smiled sadly and looked away.

I rose to my feet and thanked her. Politely she showed me out, primly and properly. I was surprised to see the shadows dark and lengthening across the bright green lawn. We'd talked longer than I'd thought.

I'd covered almost half the distance to the sidewalk before I noticed a dark green Mustang convertible parked just behind my own car. A blond teen-age boy sat motionless at the wheel, watching me as I approached.

Could it be the son, Johnny? The mother had mentioned a Mustang. And the driver was watching me with a kind of languid attentiveness, as if more than casually interested, yet unwilling to surrender to open curiosity.

But how could I begin a conversation? A newspaperman's routine questioning might be the best pose, yet I'd given his mother another story.

I stopped at the side of my car, hand on the door handle and allowed my eyes to rest fully on him. He was returning my gaze; he hadn't stirred. I frowned, as if suddenly struck by a puzzling thought. Then, pretending to act on an almost breezy impulse, I walked back to the Mustang, smiling as I went.

"Are you Johnny Hanson, by any chance?" I asked, still smiling.

"Yes," he answered in a soft, low voice. He didn't return my smile, but only looked at me with steady, inscrutable blue eyes. He was a pale, handsome boy with a serious, compressed mouth. Had Faith Hanson said sixteen?

His manner seemed much older.

"Mind if I talk to you for a minute?" I waved my hand toward the house. "I've just been talking to your mother. You might be able to help me, too."

"Help you with what?"

"Well, ah . . ." I cleared my throat. "The fact is that is that I'm investigating the, ah, murder of Dominic Vennezio, three weeks ago. Your mother knew him, I understand. And . . ." I hesitated. How much did the boy know of his mother's affair with the gangster?

"Get in if you want to," he said, moving his head toward the Mustang's passenger seat.

"Thanks." I circled the car, covertly glancing at the house. Almost without doubt, Faith Hanson was watching us.

"Are you a detective?" he asked, turning in the seat to face me.

"Private investigator," I answered, swinging the door closed.

"Were you questioning Mother about Vennezio's murder, did you say?" Now he was frowning, as if trying to comprehend.

I nodded. Then, in an effort to put him at ease, I took out my cigarettes, vainly offered him one and leisurely lit one for myself.

"Is Mother a . . ." He blinked. "A suspect?"

"No, it's nothing like that. But, as I'm sure you know, she's an important witness. She found the body. You . . ." I hesitated. "You knew that, didn't you?"

His mouth twisted into a brief, wounded mockery of a smile. "Yes, Mr. . . ." He paused, looking at me with a kind of arch elegance.

69

"Drake," I supplied. "Sorry."

He nodded gracefully. More and more, his manner was assuming a Noel Coward quality—or at least he was acting out a fair imitation.

"Thank you." He sighed, allowing his eyes to wander as he said, "Yes, Mr. Drake. I knew she'd found the body. I didn't know until I read it in the papers next morning, at school. But at least I knew."

"Well, I'm sure your mother was very upset. And, besides, she probably didn't finish with the police until late at night."

"Yes, that's what she said." He seemed to have lost interest in the conversation. For a time, I was content to sit merely smoking—studying his too-delicate profile, waiting for him to speak. I was trying to imagine what kind of a life Johnny Hanson must live, attending his boarding school in the exclusive Ojai Valley. At best, his mannerisms must often make him the butt of much teen-age humor.

At worst, I decided, he might be ensnared in the beginnings of homosexuality. Certainly his features lacked masculine solidity; certainly his loose little hand gestures and elaborate little sighs hinted at sexual ambivalence.

He was running a finger over the steering wheel, dreamily.

"He gave me this car," he said finally. "Just a month before he died. It was for my sixteenth birthday."

"Mr. Vennezio, you mean?"

He nodded.

"Did you know him very well?"

He seemed to consider his answer before saying, "Mr. Vennezio used to make it a point to see me whenever I

70

was home. He spent a lot of time pounding me on the back and asking me if there was anything I needed. He always wanted me to call him Dominic. He kept asking me out to the beachhouse, so I could meet the surfing crowd. But I never went, of course."

I couldn't think of a reply. So, instead, I decided to ask, "Do you think your mother has any idea who killed him, Johnny?"

He shook his head, still tracing the rim of the steering wheel with a reflective forefinger.

"No, I don't think Mother knows," he answered. Then he turned his eyes to mine.

"But I do," he said softly.

"You——" I swallowed. "You do?"

He nodded, still staring at me with his calm blue eyes.

"You mean you think you know who killed him?"

Again he nodded.

"Well, who—who is it?"

"The third man in her life," he answered, coyly enigmatic.

"The third man? What d'you mean?"

"Well," he said, "first there was my father. You've heard about my father, haven't you?" He looked at me with quizzical mockery.

I nodded.

"Then, after my father," he continued, "there were—several men. 'Friends.' 'Business associates.' They came and they went. Then, there was Mr. Vennezio. Just Mr. Vennezio—until finally my father left. And, for a long time, there was still just Mr. Vennezio. However, recently, there's been the third man. He was beginning to overlap Mr. Vennezio."

"And you think this third man killed him?"

71

Dreamily decisive, he said, "Yes, I do. I'm sure of it. When your mother has a long succession of—friends, you develop an instinct for these things. I'm quite sure there was a third man."

"But did you ever actually see him?"

"Not really. Not his face."

"Then you don't know his identity?"

"No."

"And your mother never admitted having another . . ." I hesitated. "Another lover?"

"How could she?" he asked. "She never even admitted that Mr. Vennezio was her lover. They were just—" his lip slightly curled. "—just good friends."

I thought about it, disappointed. It all seemed a meaningless fantasy. Yet he was willing to give me information. My obvious tactic was to get everything I could from him, then sort out fact from fancy.

"Do you have any idea where your father is, Johnny?"

"At this moment, you mean? Now?"

"Well, not—not especially right now. But I just wondered whether you'd seen him, lately. Your mother hasn't, but I thought that maybe you'd—"

"No," he said quickly, his tone slipping up to a harsh treble. "I haven't seen my father for two years. Almost exactly two years. Since he left, I haven't seen him."

"The reason I asked," I said slowly, "I was wondering whether he might be the third man. I'm not suggesting that he was the murderer. I'm just wondering whether he might've been—in the background, watching."

He promptly shook his head. "No, no. It wasn't my father."

"But how can you be so sure, if you've never seen this

person? I mean, it all seems to be a—a feeling you have. Nothing more."

"A feeling?" He arched an elaborate brow, burlesqueing a sophisticated irony.

"Well, isn't it?" I asked, suddenly irriated. "You said it yourself: you don't know his identity. And if you don't know that, then I don't see how it's possible for you to know that this—this fictitious man is the murderer. Not unless you—" I paused, struck by the thought. "Not unless you were in the habit of following your mother, at a distance, say." I looked at him closely. "Have you followed her?"

Slightly smiling, he shook his head. Teasing.

"Have you ever been to the beachouse, for instance," I pressed, "when your mother and Vennezio were there?"

He continued to shake his head, still smiling. Then, with a sigh, he glanced at his watch.

"It's five thirty," he said. "I'm afraid I have to get back to school soon."

I nodded, opening the door and stepping out of the Mustang.

"Thanks for your information, Johnny," I said. "If I can be of any help to you—or you think of anything that might help me, I'd appreciate a call. I'm staying at the Prescott Motel."

"The Prescott." He nodded. "I know where it is."

"Good. You won't forget, will you?"

"No, Mr. Drake," he answered, also getting out of the car and striding toward the house. "I won't forget."

5

I DECIDED to return to my motel, have dinner and phone Mrs. Vennezio, reporting my progress. Then I planned to watch TV for an hour or so and go to sleep. The day had left me drained, and as I ate my dinner I tried to analyze the causes. The answers, unhappily, were obvious. At ten o'clock that morning, standing in the phone booth and wrestling with my timid conscience, I'd been someone recognizable to myself: Stephen Drake, age thirty-two. Intelligence—better than average; physical courage —average or less. Lucky with some girls, unlucky with most. Physically tall and spare, with a receding hairline and dark, intense eyes, well suited to ESP publicity pictures. Vocationally I was a better-than-competent crime reporter. I had a by-line on the *San Francisco Sentinel* and a columnist's contract. I was also the grateful possessor of a modicum of modest fame. That some of my reputation as a clairvoyant derived from hokum was not really disturbing. I could honestly claim proficiency both as a reporter and as a clairvoyant, however labored and sketchy might be my private processes of ESP.

At ten o'clock that morning, therefore, I was a reasonably happy man, secure in the knowledge of my own achievements.

By noon—two short hours later—I'd become a servant of the underworld. And, worse, I'd been warned. It had all happened exactly as Captain Larsen had predicted it would.

Walking down the long corridor to my room, I was aware that I was thudding my heels angrily into the thick hallway carpeting. I'd made a fool of myself. What could I do about it? The choice was obvious: either return the thousand dollars and leave town or stay and try to earn the other nine thousand, quickly.

Nine thousand dollars . . .

Larsen had anticipated that, too. 'It always begins with money,' he'd said.

With an impatient, almost vicious twist I opened the door of my room and flipped on the light.

Mrs. Vennezio's dwarf was lounging in an easy chair, smiling.

"You should be more careful about locking up." He pointed to the room's outside door, leading to the patio and the parking lot beyond. "Someone could walk in and clean you out." He gestured reprovingly at my open suitcase and at my other things scattered around the room.

"You should be more careful, too," I retorted. "House detectives don't like their guests disturbed." As I said it, I realized that I was almost pettishly venting my frustrations—picking on someone smaller than myself, while the neighborhood bully swaggered off.

His smile faded. He sat up straighter: a small, ludicrous figure in the large chair. His feet didn't quite reach the floor.

"Maybe we should both be more careful." As he spoke, he slowly reached inside his jacket, withdrawing an ice pick. Following the gesture with a kind of numbed fascination, I watched him lightly heft the weapon. With his pale blue eyes he stared at me, unblinking. Then, in a smooth, effortless overhand motion he threw the ice pick It flashed across the room, striking the wall perhaps two inches from a large mirror. The pick didn't quiver. It entered the wall like a huge nail, driven deeply into the plaster.

Slowly the dwarf got down from his chair, walked with a lopsided gait to the opposite wall and twisted the ice pick free. For a moment he stood surveying the room. Then, with the same smooth movement, he threw the ice pick just above a large picture of a sunrise, elaborately framed. The pick struck the wall a bare inch from the picture frame. The picture hung less than two feet from where I stood.

The dwarf pointed to the ice pick.

"It's too high for me to reach." His voice was soft; his eyes never left mine. "Get it for me, will you?"

Conscious that my throat felt terribly dry, I turned toward the picture, grasped the ice pick and pulled. As I did, an inch-square piece of plaster fell to the floor.

I turned the ice pick in my hand. Handle first, I handed the weapon to the dwarf. He took it, smiled with a kind of polite, amiable wolfishness and slipped the pick inside his coat. Then he reached into his jacket pocket and withdrew a sheaf of money in his small hand.

"Here." He gestured for me to take the bills. "That's another thousand dollars. From Mrs. Vennezio."

As I took the money, I swallowed repeatedly, wishing

for a large, cool glass of water. I watched the dwarf return to his easy chair. Then, as if helpless to do anything else, I counted the money. Ten one-hundred-dollar bills. With unsteady hands, I took out my wallet.

"Why don't you sit down?" The dwarf smiled, this time with a wide, expansive warmth, almost infectious. He gestured to the bed. And, obediently, I sat.

"My name's Reggie Fay," he said pleasantly. "Mrs. Vennezio might not've told you. I'm her bodyguard. I been with them for years. Her and Mr. Vennezio, I mean." He pointed to the picture frame. "Too bad about that plaster. Maybe you can get some spackle or something. Better yet, I'll bring you some. We got some in the garage, I think."

"Tha . . ." I swallowed. "Thank you."

Airily he waved. "That's all right." He patted his jacket, where the ice pick was now concealed. "I throw that thing every day, for a half-hour, at least. Regularly. It's hard to get them with metal handles, you know. And the ones with wooden handles, they're too light to throw so they'll do much good. I sent away for this one. I bought a dozen." He smiled. "Ever since, they been sending me catalogues, and everything, about butcher supplies. They think I got a butcher shop or something."

I tried to smile, but was aware that the attempt must seem grotesque. I was wondering how many remained, of his dozen ice picks.

"How you doing?" His voice was solicitous.

"How—how do you mean?"

"I mean, how you doing? Figuring out who killed Mr. Vennezio?"

"Well, I—I haven't had a chance to do much." I took a

deep breath, reassured now by his apparent amiability. He'd demonstrated his capacity for destruction. He'd made his point. Now, possibly, he wanted to ingratiate himself.

"I hear you got Mr. Russo's O.K."

"Yes. That—that's what he said."

Reggie Fay nodded judiciously. "That's good. You got Mr. Russo pulling for you, then you got no problems. You play ball with him, he plays ball with you. But if you cross him . . ." The small man grimaced, mocking a forlorn sadness.

"Was Dominic Vennezio like that?" I asked.

"Mr. Vennezio was different. Mr. Russo, he uses his brains instead of his muscle. He keeps you guessing—a little off-balance, until he gets you in line. But not Mr. Vennezio. He was the old-fashioned kind, if you know what I mean. Anything he got, he got the hard way. That's the way he came up, and that's all he ever knew. Hit 'em on the head." Reggie Fay struck the arm of his chair a sharp, vicious blow. "Bop."

I decided to try and draw him out, not by asking questions directly, but by apparently confiding in him, enticing conversation.

"I think that's what got him killed," I said. "That bopping. I think he bopped one person too many."

"Oh, yeah?" He sat forward on the edge of his chair, gripping the arms. "How'd you figure that out? Did you see it in a mental flash, or what?"

I shook my head and smiled. "I'm not that, ah, facile, I'm afraid. I have to work for my flashes."

"I read about one of you guys. Some guy in Europe, he could tell the police exactly where to look for a kid that'd drownded a whole month before. He told the cops to go to a certain place along the riverbank on a certain day, at a certain hour. He said the kid's body would come floating up to the top. And that's what happened. He does that kind of stuff all the time. He handles something that belongs to the person, like a handkerchief, or a glove, or something. That's all he needs. He can tell what's in the future, too. Like fortune-telling."

"Well, he's luckier than I am. I have to do a lot of legwork."

"Do you see it all like a big, bright picture, or what?" His avid, intent expression was guileless—almost childlike.

At that, I had to ruefully snort.

"I see it as a very small, very muddy picture. Sometimes it's like seeing an abstract painting, that you have to figure out. Everything's there, but it's meaningless."

He nodded and thoughtfully blinked. Then, leaning sideways against the chair's arm, he tucked his feet up beside him. It was an oddly feminine posture. Suddenly he seemed vulnerable—if one could forget the ice pick tucked inside his natty tweed sport jacket.

"So you got to play detective until you get the picture. Is that it? And then you got to figure out what the picture means, sometimes."

I nodded. "Exactly."

"And that's what you're doing now. Playing detective."

"Yes. I'm asking everyone I can. Trying to piece something together. Then maybe I'll get the picture. Literally."

He cocked his head almost pertly aside, thinking about it.

"And you think Mr. Vennezio was killed by someone

he bopped too hard. Is that it?"

"That's what I think, yes. He must've had a hundred enemies. In his, ah, line of business, he could've made enemies he didn't even know existed. A cigar store owner, for instance, could've gone broke because the Outfit moved in with one of their own, ah, cigar stores."

Reggie Fay nodded thoughtfully, stroking his chin in a gesture that seemed to burlesque manhood.

"Yeah, I see what you mean. Except for one thing."

"What's that?"

"The job was too smooth. Too professional."

"The murderer could've just been lucky. It happens all the time."

He thought about it, then judiciously shook his head. "I don't know about luck, where murder's concerned. It takes more than luck. Figure it out for yourself: a guy's doing something that could mean the gas chamber. So luck's not enough."

"What does it take, then?"

"It takes experience." His manner was decisive—flat with an authoritative finality. "A job that clean, it takes experience."

"What you're saying, then, is that someone in your, ah, organization did it. Is that right?"

He shrugged. "I'm just talking about this luck thing. I'm not pointing anywhere."

"Mr. Russo says there wasn't any, ah, official beef against Vennezio."

"I wouldn't know about that. I'm low down on the pole. Real low down."

"But you were Vennezio's bodyguard."

Now his expression became ironic. He snorted. "If you

80

really want to know, I was always around mostly to mind the Vennezio kids, Angelo and Charlene." He paused and once more shrugged. "I'm forty-eight years old. I don't look it, but I am. I started with Mr. Vennezio twenty-five years ago, running errands. I could never be a bagman, or anything like that, because I was too conspicuous. So I just used to run errands. I guess Mr. Vennezio and the other big shots, they kept me around for luck or something. They were always polite, and everything—except when they'd get to drinking. Then they'd start kidding around with me. Kings, you know, used to do that." He paused, briefly trapped in a sad, distant reverie. Then, drawing a deep breath, he said, "Anyhow, when Angelo got to be two or three years old, he used to get real happy whenever I showed up. He'd clap his hands and laugh and run over to me. Charlene did the same, too, when she was old enough. So gradually I became the kids' bodyguard, sort of. When Mr. Vennezio first came out here from the East, there was lots popping, believe me. Guys were getting killed every week, until Siegel finally got it. The kids never got hurt, but you never knew. Finally, though, things calmed down, and the kids grew up. So I just kind of stayed around. Then, a couple of years ago, Mr. Vennezio's wife moved out on him, like she told you. And I went with her. To—" He hesitated. "To keep an eye out for her."

"How do you mean?" I pretended not to understand.

"You know . . ." Guilelessly-seeming now, he spread his hands. "Just keep an eye on her. Mr. Vennezio, he was pretty worried about her. He wanted to make sure she was all right."

I decided not to pursue the point. Instead, musingly, I

81

said, "The way I understand it, then, you think Vennezio was murdered by a professional, but not necessarily for, ah, professional reasons."

He thought about it, frowning. Then he finally nodded. "Yeah, I guess that's one way of putting it." His eyes were uneasy, foreshadowing evasiveness.

It was time to shift my ground.

"What about Charlene? I understand she's been going around with, ah . . ." I couldn't come up with the name.

"Larry Sabella." He was watching me carefully.

"Right. Larry Sabella. And I hear her father didn't approve."

He got to his feet. "I guess I better be going."

"Wait a minute." I also rose. "Tell me something about this Sabella. I could ask Frank," I added, by way of technique. "But I'd as soon not bother him."

Using Russo's first name seemed to have an effect. Reggie Fay turned to face me, staring up at me intently. Finally he said, "Larry Sabella runs the gambling end of things. He and Charlene are pretty thick, I guess. They have been, for three or four years."

"And Dominic didn't like it."

"No. He sure didn't. He was always real wrapped up in Charlene, the way some guys get about their daughters."

"Is Sabella married?"

"He's divorced. He got divorced just about the time he and Charlene started going around together. Maybe a little before. I'm not sure."

"Does Charlene live by herself?"

"Now she does. For the last two years, after Mr. and Mrs. Vennezio split up, she lived by herself. Before that, she lived at home."

"You said, though, that she'd gone with Sabella for three or four years."

"Yeah. She used to see him without her father knowing."

I thought I saw my chance to slip Mrs. Hanson into the conversation.

"Did Charlene know Mrs. Hanson?"

He shrugged. "She knew about her. I don't know whether they ever met. I doubt it, though."

"Did Charlene like the idea of her father having someone like Mrs. Hanson?"

His eyes became opaque, his manner noncommittal. "You'd have to ask Charlene about that."

I nodded, thinking over his answers. As I did, I realized that Reggie Fay was far from stupid. His insights were sharp and his mind quick.

I decided to try for one last bit of information.

"Do you happen to know," I began tentatively, "how Dominic left his estate? I mean, did he make a will, for instance?"

He smiled, as a card player might smile at an opponent's clumsy play.

"That's not my department, Mr. Drake." He turned and limped to the door. "About some things you can pump me. But I know when to stop talking. That's how I got to be forty-eight years old." He opened the door and politely wished me good night.

I sat for perhaps five minutes, thinking over the conversation. Then, on an impulse, I dialed Mrs. Vennezio's number. She answered the phone herself, on the second ring.

"This is Stephen Drake," I said, trying to make my voice cordial. "I just wanted to thank you for the money."

"That's all right. Have you found out anything?"

"I'm afraid not, Mrs. Vennezio. But I only got in town last night, and I haven't been able to question anyone until today. However, now, I'm beginning to get an idea of the kind of information I need."

"What kind of information is that?" It seemed a cautious question.

"Well, that's the reason I called. First, I'd like to know how your husband left his estate. Who benefited, in other words."

A long silence followed. I was on the point of repeating the question when she asked, "It's necessary, that you have this information?"

"Yes, it is, Mrs. Vennezio. Absolutely." As I said it, decisively, I realized that I may have turned a corner: demanding something of others, rather than merely awaiting their demands on me. I was dimly realizing, too, that I possessed an important advantage in my present situation—a cultural advantage. "Class" seemed to count heavily in underworld society.

". . . just left a handwritten will," Mrs. Vennezio was saying. "It was just one page, that's all. But the lawyer says it's good. It's in the probate court right now."

"What're its provisions?"

"Well, Dom said that first everything he had should be turned into cash within six months, at the best price. Then next everything but fifteen thousand dollars was to be divided three ways and given to me and the kids."

"And what about the fifteen thousand dollars?"

"Five thousand of it goes to Reggie Fay and ten thousand to that—that woman."

"I see. And what's the total estate, Mrs. Vennezio?"

"Well . . ." She hesitated. "Most of it's in real estate, but the lawyers figure it'll be around three hundred thousand dollars."

"Three hundred—that's a lot of money."

"Dominic worked hard," she replied, defensive-sounding. "And he saved his money. All our life, we only had one car. Things like that."

I thought about it, visualizing life with one Cadillac and three hundred thousand dollars in real estate.

"Were your children on good terms with their father, Mrs. Vennezio?"

A brief silence followed. Then she said, "What difference does it make, about Dominic and the kids? Do you think they know something about Dom's murder?"

"No, no," I answered hastily. "It's not that. It's just that I want to know everything I can about your husband. I have to—to fill in the picture. I have to feel that I *know* him. For example, I'm very interested in talking to your daughter, just to get her impressions."

"You want to talk to the kids, is that it?" Her voice had the same flat, resigned quality I remembered from our conversation in San Francisco.

"Yes. That's it."

A moment of silence followed. Then, reluctantly, she said, "Charlene's in the Los Angeles phone book. If you want to find out about Charlene, you'd better ask her yourself. We—Charlene and I never hit it off. Not for a long while, anyhow."

"I see." I paused, phrasing my next question.

"Has your son been out to California lately, Mrs. Vennezio?"

"Just for the funeral. But he went right back to Phoenix."

The jet time was less than two hours, I was thinking, from Phoenix to Los Angeles. An easy commute.

"Did your husband favor one child over another?" I asked.

"Dom always liked Charlene better'n Angelo," she answered with regretful gravity. "But Angelo was a better son than Charlene was a daughter. At least, that's the way it was at first. Dom would always be spoiling Charlene, and Angelo would always be trying to do things that'd get Dom's attention. At first, when Angelo was a kid, it was just mischief. Later, when he started to grow up, it was different things. You know, teen-age things. But whatever Angelo did, right or wrong, Dom never paid much attention. So, pretty soon, Angelo didn't seem to care anymore what Dom thought. At least, that's the way it always seemed to me."

"And what about Charlene? How did she treat her father?"

"Charlene could always get anything she wanted from Dom, right from the time she was two years old. By the time she was a teen-ager, she was running wild. Everyone could see it but Dom. Whatever Charlene told Dom, he'd believe. And as long as she hung around with kids whose folks had money, anything she did was all right. And all the time she was getting into—into the kind of trouble that girls can get into, Angelo was getting into real trouble."

"Was Angelo ever actually arrested?" I asked.

She snorted, bitterly mocking humor. "Angelo finally had to leave town. He was getting arrested so often that Dom just couldn't have it."

"Was he working for the Outfit, you mean? Or did he . . . ?"

"Angelo was supposed to be going to school. College. Dom had it in his head that both kids had to go to college, no matter what. He'd threaten them, and he'd bribe them. One time he offered Angelo a thousand dollars, just to get through one college semester. But it didn't do any good. The very next week, Angelo was arrested for stealing a sports car out in Beverly Hills. It got so Dom's lawyers were spending as much time on Angelo's problems as they were on Dom's."

"What about Charlene? Did she finish college?"

"She got to be a junior, and then she quit. Just quit. And Charlene's smart, too. I remember one of her teachers saying that Charlene was about the smartest girl she'd ever taught."

I found myself holding the phone slackly. There was no more to ask—no more I wanted to hear. Mrs. Vennezio's story, I was thinking, was a timeless one. In Greek tragedy it had been the story of Oedipus, or Electra. In modern America the protagonists were anonymous, but the plot remained the same—the tragedy of two generations blindly seeking a nameless fulfillment, savagely destroying each other as they searched. In ancient times the conventions of combat were traditional and often bloody. In modern times the techniques were more refined: the silent, indifferent stare, the exclusion of turned-up transistors and TVs—and the long, gleaming cars, roaring away.

I promised to let Mrs. Vennezio know if anything developed. She thanked me, and we hung up. I rose to my feet, switched on the TV and went to the medicine cabinet for my pint of bourbon, already half-finished. I was adding a splash of water when a knock sounded. Frowning, I turned down the TV and opened the inside door, leading to the hallway.

"Mr. Drake?" He was a large, gross man with a very bald head, a big nose and the practiced smile of a petty salesman. He was wearing a sweater and slippers, and as he extended his hand he said, "I'm Walter Carrigan." Apologetically he looked up and down the hallway before lowering his voice to say, "I'm from the CIIB." He nodded over my shoulder, into the room. "Could I . . . ?"

"Yes, certainly." I stepped back, then locked the door behind me. Carrigan was standing close beside me. He nodded to the windows. "Maybe you'd better . . ."

"Yes." Quickly I crossed to the window, drawing the blinds. As I did, Carrigan sat in the same chair Reggie Fay had recently vacated.

"Sorry to just drop in on you like this." He glanced around the room, completely at his ease. "But I'm just down the hall, so there didn't seem much point in phoning for an appointment." He smiled, as if pleased with the figure of speech.

"But how did you—I mean—"

"How'd we find out about you? Is that what you're asking?" He scrubbed his shaven head with a reflective hand. I noticed the thick growth of black hair on the back of his hand. Something in the contrast of the hair-matted hand and the completely smooth skin of the skull seemed almost obscene. If this was a representative of California's home-grown FBI, I was thinking, appearance could not have been a recruitment factor.

"Was it Larsen who told you?" I asked, aware of a quick indignation.

"Larsen? Who's Larsen?" Carrigan's eyes, I noticed, protruded slightly. His close scrutiny was therefore doubly distasteful.

"Never mind." I was looking at my bourbon and water, which I'd placed on the dresser. I wanted the rest of the drink, but I didn't want to offer one to my unwelcome visitor. The TV screen, mute, was announcing a panel show.

"Who's Larsen?" he repeated.

"Chief of Homicide in San Francisco," I answered shortly, remembering that Larsen had emphatically warned me to stay clear of both the CIIB and the FBI. The warning had left a graphic vision in my mind: the image of myself face down on the floor of Frank Russo's car.

"Oh, yeah," came the answer. "I think I've heard about him. Supposed to be a good man."

I nodded, trying to decide how best to get rid of him. If he were known to the Outfit . . .

"I came down from Sacramento," he said, as if to answer my unspoken question. "Our L.A. office thought it would be best if they didn't contact you."

"Well, that . . ." I shifted in my chair, glancing at the drawn blinds. "That's very considerate of you. And wise, too," I added. "I've been told that there'd be, ah, considerable risk if . . ." I didn't know how to finish it. Among law enforcement officers, I realized, the Outfit was seldom referred to directly. Correct form was to officially ignore the existence of organized crime when speaking for the record—or when speaking to the representative of another official organization.

Stirring the flabby folds of his face into an unconvincing smile, Carrigan raised a foot from the floor. "That's why I'm wearing these slippers. To minimize the risk to you."

"Yes, but . . ." Involuntarily I glanced at the outside door, through which Reggie Fay had disappeared less than ten minutes before.

"Does Russo know you're staying here at the Prescott?" His tone had now flattened to a brusk, official note.

"Yes, he does. That's why I—"

"Have you had a chance to talk with Russo yet?"

"Yes. Today. This morning."

"What'd he say?"

"Listen, Mr. Carrigan." I leaned toward him, lowering my voice. "One of the things Russo said was that I was to stay away from the police. Or it'd be my neck, he implied. Now, I talked to Larsen about all this before I ever left San Francisco. He advised me not to come to Los Angeles, and I can see now that he was right. But I'm here now, and I don't have much choice but to—"

"I disagree with Larsen. I don't see anything wrong with you being here. Just be sure you keep us posted, that's all. You're a crime reporter. You should know we protect our informers from—"

"Look, let me call you on the phone. Give me a number, and I promise I'll report once a day, at least. But, for God's sake, I don't think you should—"

"Now, listen, Drake. The way I understand this deal, you're being paid a bundle of money to find out who killed Dominic Vennezio. Then . . ." He held up two spread fingers. "Then, second, you're being paid not to tell anyone about it. Any of the authorities, I mean. Now—" He shook his head, in ponderous burlesque of a regretful reproach. "Now, that just isn't the way we want to see it happen, Drake. We don't mind if you give the information to Russo. He's paying for the information, and he's got a right to get it. However, if you uncover any information relative to the murder of Dominic Vennezio, you're going to be in real hot water with the law if you don't—"

"But Russo's not paying me. It's Mrs. Vennezio. She's the one I'm working for. She—"

"She's a front for Russo. You know it, and so do I." His protuberant eyes were chilled; his voice was barbed with a policeman's cynical, bored contempt. As a reporter, I'd often heard that note of contempt in a cop's voice, questioning a suspect.

"She's not a front," I protested. "She's—"

"You're reporting to Russo, though."

"Well, yes. But——"

"He says 'no,' it's no."

I sighed. "Listen, Carrigan, what you're saying is right. But don't forget this: the whole La Palada police department is jumping to Russo's tune. It's not just me. In fact, I'm a lot more independent than—"

"All right, Drake. There's no point in arguing. You can talk all you want to, but I'm telling you what's going to happen. Now, if you want to phone in once a day, that's

91

fine. I'll give you a number you can use, downtown. However, I'm also going to keep an eye on you. For one thing, assuming you really do turn up something, you might need some help. For another, still assuming you turn up something, there's a little matter of what constitutes evidence. You might tell the jury, for instance, that you talked with Frankie Russo or Larry Sabella. But Russo and Sabella might say you didn't. If you had a witness, though—a well-concealed witness, who was also a law officer—things might turn out a lot different in court. Of course," he added in a patronizing tone, faintly contemptuous, "we wouldn't expect you to testify in court. As I said, we protect our sources."

"Thanks for that, anyhow." I made no effort to conceal the hostile irony in my voice. Informers, like certain lower insects, could not sustain themselves in the full light of day.

Yet, in the next moment, I realized I'd never have the courage to testify against the Outfit. Score one, I thought, for Carrigan—and another for Larsen.

He shrugged and got ponderously to his feet.

"You're the one who decided to play with the big boys, Drake. Nobody forced you." He took a small notebook from his pocket, scribbled and tore out a slip of perforated paper. "Here's the phone number. Ask for me, then identify yourself as my . . ." He paused. ". . . my friend from Portland. Don't mention your name or any other names connected with the case, and always use a pay phone. We'll call Russo the first subject and Sabella the second subject. Any questions?"

I shook my head.

"Good." He moved briskly to the door, unlocked it, and

stepped out into the corridor, softly closing the door behind him.

I slipped the perforated slip of paper into my billfold, snapped off the TV and absently reached for my drink. Then I crossed the room and drew open the blinds. Propping a foot on the low windowsill, I stared morosely out into the night. The lights of Los Angeles were diffused by the city's inevitable smog, reducing the harsh neon brightness of sign shapes to the softness of pastel abstractions, disembodied in the darkness.

What could I do?

The question seemed almost academic, because the problem was so impossibly complex. I remembred the difficulty I'd had learning chess. To each thrust there was a possible counterthrust—then an answering thrust to the counterthrust, and so on and on. This problem was the same. Russo could check Carrigan, but Carrigan could checkmate Russo—provided Carrigan himself could escape from check. And both men could eliminate me upon the merest whim, because both represented vast forces within society, just as did bishops and knights and kings and queens on the chessboard. By comparison, I was a pawn—a vassal, indentured for the most menial work. I sought merely money—eight thousand dollars more.

Eight thousand dollars—more than some people saved in a lifetime.

I sighed, straightened and blinked my eyes into focus. I must think. I must analyze the problem, clearly and concisely—once and for all.

Probably because I had a college diploma, Frank Russo liked me. Yet Russo was a businessman. He was responsible for the efficient functioning of a large, complicated enterprise engaged in the very serious business of narcotics, prostitution and gambling. Therefore, Russo could not permit a personal whim to alter company policy or to compromise company discipline. He must . . .

Beyond the window, the pastel tints of faded neon dissolved into the velvet darkness of a deeper night. Stars shown brilliantly in the sky; beneath the stars curved the surf, a phosphorescent tracery along the dark, deserted beach. The structure stood stark against the sky—the house with the lighted door. In the doorway stood the stocky, stolid silhouette of a man, staring sightlessly out into the night, listening.

Nearby stood the woman, silent and watching. She was draped in a coarsely woven cloak, falling in long Gothic folds to the sand at her feet. She stood motionless, her face concealed by the cowl of her cloak. They were alone in the night: the man in the doorway, listening—and the still figure on the beach, waiting.

Then, slowly, a third figure approached, emerging from the surrounding night like a silent, furtive actor leaving the darkened wings to take his place on a dimly lit stage. The third figure stealthily drew closer to the man in the doorway. Now the woman on the beach raised her arm in some slow, imperious command. The third figure suddenly tensed, crouching—scrabbling for a close-by concealment. The man in the doorway was turning, seeking escape—slowly, dreamily lifting first one leg, then the other—running in the agonized suspension of a nightmare, helplessly. One stride, two. The man was smaller now in the orange rectangle of the doorway light, escaping. But now the third figure stepped again quickly into full view, and in that instant the running man halted in midstride, frozen. Then he fell, stricken. The movement was surrealistically slow, as if his lifeless body were suspended by invisible strings, gently collapsing.

As the body finally lay inert, the orange rectangle of light faded into the surrounding darkness.

6

ALL THROUGH that Sunday night the vision of the three tortured figures writhed in my twisted dreams, leaving me sleepless and exhausted when morning finally came. It was a sensation I'd often experienced during the past few years. What had I actually seen? What had I imagined? What did it all mean? If the one lifeless figure was Dominic, who were the other two—the faceless woman and the furtive assassin? Was it all a meaningless fantasy, signifying nothing? It had happened before.

Was it a fantasy? Pure imagination?

Until I either identified the two figures, or proved them false, I would never know.

Wearily I got out of bed, showered, dressed and had breakfast. I had decided to phone Charlene Vennezio, and at nine thirty I dialed her number. From her manner I was sure she'd already heard of my arrival in Los Angeles, and as we talked I felt as if I were an especially unwelcome salesman, begging a reluctant prospect for an appointment. Finally, in a brusk voice, almost rudely, she said I could come to her apartment just after lunchtime.

The apartment building was a new stone-and-glass structure, and as I entered the lobby I decided that the rent for one of the larger apartments would probably exceed my monthly reporter's salary. Her apartment was on the tenth floor, and as I pressed the button marked "C. Vennezio" I could hear a voice inside. Then, abruptly, the door came open. A tall, dark-haired girl dressed in slim-tapered slacks and a man's white shirt stared at me appraisingly as I introduced myself. Then she turned back into the room.

"Come in," she said over her shoulder. "I'm on the phone. Sit down."

I closed the hallway door behind me, and followed her into the living room. She stood in front of a huge plate glass window, holding the phone in her hand, trailing a long cord. Even though her back was turned to me, exasperation was plain in her stance as she listened for a moment before saying into the phone:

"I'll tell you one more time, Mr. Leonard: That car was promised for ten o'clock this morning, and it's now one o'clock in the afternoon. I'll also remind you that the car is still on warranty. Now, I'm leaving this afternoon for a trip. I either want that car ready, or I want one just like it. And I don't mean a used car, either. If you can't get my car fixed, I want a demonstrator. And I— What?"

She listened impatiently, then said, "I don't know anything about vapor locks, Mr. Leonard. I just know about warranties, and the Better Business Bureau." She dropped the receiver into the phone's cradle, pivoted and deposited the phone on a small side table. For a long moment she stood in the center of the room, looking down at me as I sat on her sofa. Then, unexpectedly, she

97

smiled.

"So you're my mother's own private clairvoyant?" Her voice was lightly derisive. She moved back to lean against a low credenza, half sitting—stretching out her long, elegant legs. Something in Charlene Vennezio's disdainful assurance and restless vitality reminded me of Carmen. *Fiery* was the word Mrs. Hanson had used. It seemed an accurate adjective.

"My name is Drake," I said, irritated at her flippancy. "Stephen Drake."

She nodded, still derisively smiling. "That's what you said in the hallway. And on the phone, too. It seems to me that I read something about you a few years ago. Something about solving the murder of a very important man. Was that you?"

I shrugged. "It depends on who the man was. It could have been me."

Her smile faded. "So now you're going to do the same for us. Is that right?"

Again I shrugged, and decided not to answer. I was wishing that she'd sit down in a chair and get to the business at hand. She had a disturbing effect on me, with her legs braced straight out and her torso arched upward as she leaned back against the credenza.

"There was a time," she said abruptly, "when I was interested in psychology, including ESP. In fact psychology was the only thing I ever took in school that really interested me." Suddenly she straightened, then paced with long strides to a nearby easy chair, sitting to face me. Now she crossed her legs.

"Have you ever studied psychology, Mr. Drake?" she asked.

98

I didn't like the conversation's direction. She was questioning me, instead of my questioning her. I pointed to the phone.

"I overheard you say that you're leaving this afternoon an a trip. I wouldn't want to—"

"I just said that. Everyone says they're going on a trip when they're trying to get a car repaired. Don't you?"

"Well, I—"

"Maybe not," she interrupted, her expression one of mixed amusement and easy disdain. "You seem to be a very mild-mannered man, Mr. Drake, in spite of your imposing height and your *lean, dark good looks.*" Ironically she accented the phrase, smiling. "Did you ever know," she added, "that tall men are more successful in business than small men? Statistically, at least, height is more important than anything else to a man, even intelligence."

"Really?" In spite of myself, I was interested.

She nodded, now lightly mocking me, still smiling. "Really. With a girl, of course, it's the opposite. The smaller you are the more a man thinks he can dominate you. So, for a girl, being small is being successful. Because that's how you get a man to make love to you. Then, with luck, you get him to marry you."

"Did you learn that in psychology class?" I asked, still striving for the initiative.

"No, I didn't learn that in psychology, Mr. Drake. Anything I've ever learned, that's meant anything, I've learned by just keeping my eyes open, my mouth shut and my highball glass half-filled."

She smiled, perhaps appreciating her own flip little quip.

99

"I understand you're an actress, Miss Vennezio."

She snorted. "In my last picture I handed a mirror to the leading lady and then combed her hair. In the picture before that, I handed Gregory Peck a cocktail and thanked him when he gave me a tip."

I smiled. "At least you had some lines. I understand that's a big step forward."

She didn't reply, but was now gazing out the window, turned half away. The sky was a clear, bright blue. Two jets were tracing a parallel pattern of white vapor trails as they sped together out toward the ocean.

Watching Charlene Vennezio's dark, moody profile, I decided to come directly to the point, perhaps surprising her into a quick reaction.

"Do you have any idea who killed your father, Miss Vennezio?"

For a moment she didn't move, nor did her expression change. Yet I thought I saw her body become momentarily more rigid. Then she turned to face me.

"I thought you were going to tell me who killed him." Now her voice was no longer light, nor sardonic. Her manner seemed suddenly almost bitterly cutting, picking a fight.

I shook my head. "It's better not to tell people everything you know. The police taught me that."

"Oh." She nodded mockingly. "The police."

It had been a mistake. A gangster's daughter would never be cowed at the mention of the police. If anything, her normal response would be derisive.

"Do you have any idea who killed him?" I repeated.

"No, Mr. Drake," she answered steadily, meeting my eyes. "No, I don't."

"A suspicion, then. Anything. You were very close to your father, I understand. If anyone has an idea why he was killed, I'd think it would be you."

"Who told you that I was close to my father?" The question seemed to come with an effort.

"Your mother."

"Oh." She once more turned to stare out the window. "And how is Mother? I haven't seen her for two weeks, at least."

"She's feeling very . . ." I hesitated. "Very lonely, it seems to me."

She laughed. It was a brief, bitter sound.

"Mother's always felt lonely, as long as I've known her. She should've married a—a fruit peddler. That's what her father was, a fruit peddler."

"How did your parents happen to get married?" I asked, willing to go along with her.

"Mother was a beautiful Italian girl who came to America when she was eleven, but by the time she was seventeen she still couldn't speak English without a thick accent. She spent most of her time going to church, because her papa decided church was the safest place for Italian girls who were beautiful. Then, one day, my father saw her. Daddy was a rising young hoodlum in those days. He took one look at Mother, and decided it was true love. Her papa wasn't so sure, but it didn't take Daddy long to convince him. One visit. A semiofficial visit, the way I understand it. So they were married, and her papa ended up a prosperous fruit peddler, instead of a dead one."

"Oh." I couldn't think of anything else to say for the moment. Then, lamely, I added, "Well, that's the way they used to court in Sicily, the way I understand it."

The mocking note returned to her voice. "That's it exactly, Mr. Drake. That's how they did it in the old country. And they're still at it. You'd be surprised."

"Is that the way your father courted Mrs. Hanson?"

She looked at me sharply, her expression now cautious and shrewdly speculative.

"Why do you say that?"

I shrugged, at the same time trying to assess her reaction. A "semiofficial visit," she'd said. Had such visits been a habit with Dominic Vennezio?

"Did you know Mrs. Hanson?" I asked, watching her closely.

"I've met her. Twice. Both times accidentally."

"But you knew about your father's affair with her."

She nodded.

"And you didn't approve."

Her manner pretended a blasé indifference as she said, "If Daddy wanted to recapture his lost youth, it was his business. As long as he didn't make a fool of himself."

"But he *did* make a fool of himself, according to what I hear."

"That's a matter of opinion. Daddy was a very vital person. Everyone makes a fool of himself, sooner or later, over the opposite sex."

I was thinking about Dominic's semiprofessional visit to his intended bride's father, long ago, as I said, "I take it that you didn't know Mrs. Hanson's husband."

"No." The answer came quickly, as if she'd been waiting for the question.

"But you knew who he was."

For a long, silent moment she looked at me. Then she sighed and sat up straighter in her chair. Looking off

102

across the room, she pitched her voice to a speculative note as she said, "I suppose there's really no harm in telling you."

"No harm in telling me what, Miss Vennezio?"

She shifted in her chair to face me fully. Her manner became crisper and more businesslike. "I suppose you've heard about my, ah, friendship with Larry Sabella."

I nodded.

"You've probably also heard that Daddy didn't approve."

"Yes."

"You might also know that Daddy made a hell of a stink about me and Larry. I think he even had Larry beat up, once, by men who were supposed to be 'competitors.' Larry doesn't think so, because he always liked Daddy, or at least respected him. But I think Daddy had him beat up. Anyhow, I decided to do what I could to take some of the heat off Larry, as we say in the movies."

"And what did you decide to do?"

"I decided to let Daddy know that I knew about Mr. Hanson's strange disappearance."

I was aware of a sudden stifling sense of excitement as I asked, "What did you know about Mr. Hanson's disappearance?"

"I knew that Daddy forced him to leave town."

"How?"

"He offered him money to go. Ten thousand dollars."

"And he took it? And left?"

"Not at first. He had his pride, apparently—his drunken, patrician pride. But then Daddy explained that he had no choice. Either he left with the ten thousand dollars, or he left anyhow. Without the money."

"And what if he didn't leave?"

She moved her shoulders in a single, eloquent movement of inevitability, at the same time shaking her head.

"What did you intend to accomplish, Miss Vennezio, once your father knew that you were aware of the reasons for Mr. Hanson's leaving town?"

"Simple blackmail," she answered promptly. "If Daddy didn't quit making it tough for Larry and me, I'd blow the whistle on him to his girl friend."

"Then you don't think she knew about the ten thousand dollars."

"I don't think she knew anything. As far as she was concerned, her husband just walked out on her. Because of his wounded masculine pride, or something. Anyhow, I do know that Daddy wanted her to think her husband walked out. Very much."

"How can you be so sure?"

"Because Daddy started squirming when he heard my proposition. Then he got mad. Finally he went along. I even got him to give Larry a bigger cut. A kind of junior partnership."

I thought about Dominic Vennezio's problems with his womenfolk, and I must have smiled.

"What's the matter?" she asked resentfully.

"I was just thinking," I replied, "that you and your mother were making it pretty tough on Dominic. Apparently he didn't have much trouble keeping the toughest guys in town under his thumb. But he wasn't so lucky at home."

"What d'you mean? What're you talking about?"

"I mean that your mother was blackmailing him, too."

"Why?" she asked incredulously.

104

"Can't you guess?"

She thought about it. "Because of the Hanson woman, you mean?"

"Exactly."

She smiled, unexpectedly. "Well, good for Mother. Maybe she learned something after all, during all those years. Did she have the same information I had, about Mr. Hanson?"

"No. Her information was—different."

She didn't press the point, but instead relaxed back into her chair, pulling up her legs. She began absently tapping a forefinger on the arm of her chair. I watched her for perhaps a full half-minute, deciding what to say next. Finally, without any real plan, I started speaking:

"You know, Miss Vennezio," I said slowly, "most of my successes in the art of criminology are the result of work —lots of legwork and lots of talking, and lots more legwork. I can't say I've finished all my legwork, but I've certainly done a lot of thinking about your father's murder. And I always come back to the same problem."

"What's that?" Her voice was oddly subdued.

"A motive," I answered, watching her as I spoke.

"I shouldn't think that'd be a problem. I can think of several."

"Exactly. So can I. But that's the point: there're plenty of possible motives, but nothing that seems any more convincing than any of the others. For example, there's the obvious fact that getting murdered, in your father's business, was an occupational hazard. However, because of his position, the murder would normally be a contract job, as they call it—and a pretty big contract, at that. Now, as nearly as I can see, nothing like that happened. I

105

talked to Russo for a long time yesterday. And I'm convinced that your father's murder wasn't ordered by the Outfit."

"There's always the lone assassin." Her eyes and her voice were perfectly expressionless. She wasn't suggesting a possibility, she was merely making a minimal response.

"That's true, there's the lone assassin—possibly a nut, or even a maniac. About that, you could certainly be right." As I said it, I thought of the previous night's vision. She could be right—making me wrong. "But," I went on, "even assuming it was a lone assassin, we're still stuck for a motive. Or, at least, I'm stuck. For instance—" I held up three fingers. "Everyone agrees there're three main reasons for premeditated murder: love, revenge or the possibility of gain. Now—" I paused, organizing the lie I'd already prepared. "Now, love doesn't seem to be a factor. As far as I know, there wasn't anyone else besides your father who was romantically interested in Mrs. Hanson. Revenge, of course, is a possibility. Undoubtedly there were many people with a grievance against your father. However, at the moment, there doesn't seem to be any outstanding candidate—or at least none that I've been able to uncover. So . . ." I hesitated. "So that seems to leave the possibility of gain. Now, to me, the possibility of gain looks like the most likely motive."

She didn't reply, but only watched me with dark, expressionless eyes. She still remained curled back in the chair, but now the lines of her body seemed subtly more tense.

"For instance," I continued, "I talked to your mother last night and asked her about your father's will. She said that she, you, and your brother shared equally in the

106

bulk of the estate, with the exception of ten thousand dollars to Mrs. Hanson and five thousand to Reggie Fay. Is that right?"

She cleared her throat, seemed about to speak, but finally only nodded. I decided to veer away from the subject, perhaps to return later, unsuspected.

"Of course, there's also the possibility of someone within the Outfit gaining by your father's death," I said. "Forgetting about any high level decision to have him killed, there're probably a half-dozen men who benefited directly from Dominic Vennezio's death—just as the executives in any large company move up when the head man dies. Russo, for instance, obviously profited. And . . ." I paused. "And Larry Sabella, probably."

As I said it, I saw her eyes narrow. She returned my gaze with a kind of calm, thoughtful malice.

"It seems like you've got a pretty good parlay in Larry and me, then. Both of us profited by my father's death."

"I haven't talked to Sabella," I answered, as steadily as I could. "For all I know, he could've been out of town when the murder was committed."

"He wasn't though. He was with me. Here."

"Then there's no problem, Miss Vennezio. For either one of you."

"That's right, Mr. Drake. No problem." She was staring at me with sullen defiance. I'd seen that expression in the eyes of a hundred hoods, handcuffed to a hundred cops.

"Who do you think killed him, Miss Vennezio?" I asked quietly. "You must have some idea—some suspicion."

In the taut, hostile silence we watched each other. Then, slowly, she said, "I can't help you, Mr. Drake. As we say in the movies, all I know is what I read in the papers. I'll say this, though: Daddy undoubtedly thought he was opening the door for Mrs. Hanson instead of for his murderer. Whoever killed him arrived in her place. Think that over, Mr. Drake. Whoever killed him was . . ."

The doorbell interruped her. She rose from the chair in long, lithe movement, and quickly crossed the room to open the door.

A tall man entered with the sure, confident stride of possession.

Here, I realized, was Larry Sabella. Obviously, she'd been expecting him—waiting for him.

"This is Mr. Drake," she said with a supercilious little flourish. "The man we've all been hearing so much about. And this," she said to me, "is Mr. Larry Sabella. We thought maybe he could give you some background material for your hallucinations."

I'd risen involuntarily to my feet, facing him. As I did, I saw Charlene pick up her purse and, without a word or backward glance, leave the apartment.

"I guess she needs some cigarettes, or something," Sabella said, mockingly smiling as he advanced to the middle of the room, unconsciously striking a pose. He was one of those narcissistically handsome men, completely preoccupied with his own rugged good looks. His dark, curly hair was worn long and carefully combed. His Italian sweater was draped with casual elegance; his slacks were meticulously pressed; his loafers were beautifully burnished.

"Sit down," he said, gesturing to the chair I'd just left. Again he gave me the smile, as superficial and mannered as his posing.

I decided, immediately, that I didn't like Larry Sabella. Looking back, I realize that I'd chosen him as the focus for the frustrations, anxieties and downright terror I'd experienced during the past twenty-four hours. And, besides, phonies have somehow never much worried me.

"Want a drink?" he asked.

"No, thanks."

"How about some coffee?"

"No. I've got to be going soon."

"Oh, yeah? Where're you going?"

"I'm not really sure."

"Or else you won't tell me."

I shrugged.

With thumb and forefinger he thoughtfully arranged his trouser creases. "I hear you saw Russo yesterday," he said softly.

"That's right." I decided to light a cigarette—also deciding not to offer one to Sabella.

"Who else've you seen?" His smile had faded; the tone of his voice suggested a practiced intimidation.

I drew on the cigarette, considering. Finally, deliberately, I said, "Mr. Russo told me that I was supposed to report directly to him. And he warned me that I'd better remember it."

Sabella gave his creases a final small tug, then slowly raised his head to stare at me. With a small shock, I saw that his face had completely changed—darker, with muscles taut and bunched, eyes snapping in sudden, suppressed fury. It was as if his actor's smile had been a fragile mask now torn away, revealing a sadistic brutality.

"Russo isn't here now. Just you and me. And I'm asking

you who else you've seen."

"And I'm—" I was forced to pause and clear my throat. "And I'm telling you, Mr. Sabella, that I have orders to report to Russo—and to Russo only. Now . . ." Uncertainly, I realized, I pointed to the nearby phone. "Now, if you want to call up your boss and clear it with him, I'll gladly tell you all I know. But until then, I'm afraid I—"

"Listen, Drake," he interrupted, "don't give me this crap about clearing it with Russo. In the first place, friend, you're a little out of your own territory down here—and a little out of your depth, too. I hear, though, that you're a crime reporter. If you are and if you know your job, you should realize that there's . . ." He paused, searching for the right phrase. "There's a lot going on, down here. Lots that you don't know about—and lots that maybe Russo doesn't know about, either. Now . . ." He raised a slow, threatening forefinger, in a gesture similar to Russo's the day before. "Now, if that gets back to Russo, from you, I'll break both your legs for you. I'll deny it, of course, to Russo. But I'll break both your legs. And don't make the mistake of thinking that's just a threat. I've given it a lot of thought. I wouldn't kill you, because it's bad business, killing cops and newspapermen. But I would break both your legs. Then we'd put you in a car and run you into a tree. And if you know what's good for you, you'd tell the police it was an accident —and they'd believe you." He spread his hands, smiling his actor's smile—adjusting the mask with practiced ease. "Clear?" he asked.

I managed to keep my eyes on his. I didn't reply, but finally was compelled to nod.

He returned my nod. "Good. So let's have it. What've

110

you found out, about Vennezio's death?"

"Nothing," I answered. "Not one thing, that'd interest you. I've only talked with Faith Hanson and—" I waved a hand around the room. "—and to Miss Vennezio, just now. And neither one of them gave me any information that you probably don't have already."

"You talked to Russo, too. What'd he say?"

I sighed. Somehow I didn't really fear him—perhaps because I'd taken an instant dislike to him. I didn't doubt that he had the means and the capacity to break my legs—or even to have me killed. But, strangely, it didn't worry me. Perhaps I was experiencing a delayed reaction to the fear I'd recently felt—a kind of confused, exhausted exasperation, completely irrational. Some called it courage; others called it a coward's blind, violent protest to his own terror. I'd seen it happen often, in Korea. I'd felt it in myself.

"Russo said," I replied, "that he didn't know who killed Vennezio. He didn't think it was a—a professional job, but he wasn't sure. He's willing to find out, though, providing the authorities don't get the information first."

Inscrutably he nodded. Now the smile was a private one—and as ugly as his unmaked face.

"What'd the Hanson woman say?" he asked.

"She just repeated the story she told to the police. She didn't—"

"She knows a lot more than she's telling," he interrupted. "A hell of a lot more."

"Well, is she does, she hasn't told me. I'm no FBI man, you know. If she doesn't want to tell me anything, she doesn't have to."

"Did you talk to anyone else? Besides Charlene and

111

Faith Hanson?"

"Well . . ." I hesitated, remembering the strange, pale face of Johnny Hanson.

"Well, what? Who was it?"

"I talked to Mrs. Hanson's son. Briefly."

"Oh, yeah? Well, what'd he say? Briefly."

I drew a deep breath. For a brave moment I was tempted to refuse an answer. But finally I replied, "He said that he thought his mother had another lover, besides Vennezio."

As soon as I said it, Sabella seemed to relax, as if he'd carefully rehearsed me in a speech I'd just delivered perfectly.

"Did he say who the guy was?"

"No, he didn't."

Sabella rose, standing above me.

"Well, Drake," he said softly, "there I think I can help you. The man you're looking for . . ." He paused, for the effect. "The man happens to be my boss."

"You mean . . .?"

He nodded. "That's right. Russo. For some time, now, he's had quite a yen for Mrs. Hanson."

He turned and walked to the door. "You're doing better than I thought, Drake," he said from across the room. Then, about to open the door, he paused, turning back to face me fully.

"Don't forget," he said softly, his voice friendly and almost fey, "don't forget about those two broken legs, now. And don't forget to lock up, when you leave."

He opened the door and disappeared.

7

I LEFT Charlene Vennezio's apartment just after two
o'clock, and from a roadside phone booth called Dick
Gross, an old friend and colleague, recently elevated to
featured crime reporter on the *Los Angeles Advance*. He
agreed to meet me for coffee at three thirty, which gave
me a comfortable margin in which to cross Los Angeles,
lose myself twice on the freeway and still make the appointment with time to spare.

Despite the twenty-odd years he'd spent recording the
human capacity for vice, depravity and violence, Dick
was a cheerful optimist. His quick gray eyes, crew-cut
graying hair, ebullient disposition and pixie's sense of
wry, subtle humor seemed to reflect the successful sales
manager's view of life rather than the crime reporter's. As
we settled down to face each other across our coffee and
doughnuts, Dick spoke first:

"My paid informants have passed the word that you
and Big Frankie have been hoisting highballs beside the
pool of his $50,000 home overlooking scenic La Palada."

I was surprised. I'd been in town less than forty-eight
hours.

"So," he continued briskly, "I've decided to do a feature story on your collaboration with organized crime. My headline'll be *Journalist Takes Services to a Higher Bidder*. The story's in rewrite at this very moment."

I swallowed. "You're joking."

"Precisely." He bit into his doughnut. "I'm joking. You hope."

"Come on now, Dick. I've got enough on my mind without playing word games."

He waved a hand, smiling. "You blanched, old boy. You really blanched. If we weren't drinking buddies—or if I had any suspicion that you were going to try and stick me with this coffee and these doughnuts—I'd certainly work up a story on you. After all . . ." He gave me a brief sidelong glance. "After all, I haven't had a really crowd-pleasing story for more than three weeks. Ever since Dominic Vennezio got neatly shot three times in the chest."

"You want a refill?" I asked, pointing to his empty cup.

"As a matter of fact, I do. My wife is going to her bridge club this afternoon. And that means one thing: tuna fish salad."

"You'd better have another doughnut, then."

"Thanks, I will." He gave the order to the waitress, looked at his watch and then said, "How can I help you, old clairvoyant buddy?"

I grimaced as I finished my coffee.

"You still don't like that phrase, eh?" he said.

"No, I don't."

"That's because you're a creation of mass media, my boy. Like movie actresses. Do you know what directors

114

pointed offices?"

"No."

call movie actresses in the privacy of their lushly ap-

"It's just as well. Somehow, Steve, you've managed to retain more of your innocence than most. Perhaps that's the secret of your success. I've always been very interested in the plight of the village idiot. The townsfolk think he's in touch with the netherworld, because his mind's uncluttered by temporal considerations. Maybe they're right. Maybe you're——"

"Come on, Dick. I told you: I'm too jumpy to play games with you."

"I can see that. However, you've recovered some of your color, after my innocent little sally."

"Do you know anyone in the local CIIB?" I asked abruptly.

"Certainly."

"The head man?"

"Among others."

"Well, listen, do me a favor and ask him to take his boy off my tail."

"Who's the boy?"

"A creep named Carrigan."

"Carrigan?" He frowned. "There's no Carrigan in this office. Not unless he's a junior file clerk."

"He operates out of Sacramento."

He shook his head. "You're out of luck, friend. This Carrigan probably outranks the local bureau chief—or at least they're coequals. Are you talking about Russo and company? Is that Carrigan's assignment?"

"I guess so. Either that, or Vennezio's murder."

"Could be both. If they could hang Vennezio's murder

115

on Russo, this Carrigan would probably be running for governor next election."

I thought about Carrigan's repulsive profile, but decided to let it pass.

"How'd you happen to get mixed up in all this, Steve?" For the first time his voice was serious—or at least not flippant.

As briefly as I could, I told him. When I finished he slowly nodded, absently folding and refolding his napkin.

"I've always felt," he said finally, "that it's really money that conquers all. Love might have some appeal to the very young, but in the long run money talks. As one of the characters in your narrative observed."

"I guess I'm not in any position to argue the point."

"No," he answered quietly. "No, you're really not."

I sighed. Then, still as concisely as possible, I told him everything that I'd discovered or suspected since arriving in Los Angles. Finally, after some hesitation, I finished with a description of last night's vision.

"Well, graphically that's very good," he said judiciously. "I like that bit about the woman in the long, flowing cloak. That scans."

"Listen, Dick—"

"So now you want my theory on the murder of Dominic Vennezio," he continued. "Is that it?"

"Yes, that's it exactly."

"Well, I can give it to you in one concise, quotable statement. I don't think it was a contract job. However, contract job or not, the Outfit obviously doesn't want the La Palada police loitering around their executive suite a moment longer than's necessary to preserve appearances. So, as a result, the murder will probably never be solved, simply because the Outfit doesn't want it investigated. Not, at least, until you arrived on the scene. And if you want my private, unprofessional opinion, I think Russo's simply indulging a whim where you're concerned. Either that, or he's throwing a bone to Mrs. Vennezio. Or maybe, in view of his alleged attraction to Mrs. Hanson, he's trying to run a bluff."

"How do you mean?"

"Well, let's assume for the moment that Johnny Hanson's somewhat dubious testimony is true. Let's assume there's another man in Faith Hanson's life. Then let's assume that this man is, in fact, Russo. Now, if those two assumptions—however farfetched—are the real goods, then we've got a very interesting situation. Russo has got himself involved in precisely the same jackpot that Vennezio manufactured for himself, presumably to the consternation of the Outfit. As everyone knows, the Outfit doesn't like scandal. Russo is vulnerable, in other words —just like Vennezio was vulnerable. So that, if there's some kind of an intramural power-play afoot, possibly featuring Larry Sabella as the young Turk, then Russo's got to protect himself. So, when you arrive on the scene so ingenuously, Russo's got a choice: either send you packing, and perhaps strengthen Sabella's hand, or try to bluff it out. Now, let's say he decides to bluff it out. Maybe he wants time while he arranges a transfer for Sabella to the Des Moines office. Meanwhile, to keep the light touch, he acts amused at your poor efforts. He invites you to do your meager best—being careful to make very sure you report everything to him. See?"

"Yes," I answered slowly. "That's all occurred to me. On the other hand, as you suggest, there's always the possibility that both Johnny Hanson and Larry Sabella are nothing more than troublemakers."

"To me," Gross answered, "that's the most likely construction. Unless young Hanson can come up with something more than adolescent mysticism, you can't put too much stock in what he says. As for Sabella, he's young and ambitious. Most people think he took up with Vennezio's daughter out of pure ambition—in spite of the fact that he was running considerable risk. So when you tell me that after hearing of this alleged second lover Sabella identified him as Russo, I'd be inclined to say it was pure spur-of-the-moment opportunism."

"You haven't heard anything about it through the grapevine, then?"

"Absolutely not."

"Have you heard anything unofficial down at headquarters about Vennezio's murder?"

He shook his head. "Negative. You know as well as I do, everyone in law enforcement would like to pretend the Outfit doesn't exist. Most of the time they succeed. Brilliantly."

"But you must've heard something."

He thought about it before saying, "Well, one friend of mine on the Los Angeles force seems to think there's a personal motive involved. Something in Vennezio's love life, which we've already covered, or his family or his past."

"What about Vennezio's son?"

"Angelo?" He snorted. "I doubt it. Angelo's one of these hysterical tough guys; he's not for real. And, believe me, whoever pulled the trigger on Dominic had to be for real. Angelo is a punk, nothing more and nothing less. The Mafia blood thins rapidly, you know. Apparently it can't stand long exposure to the American way of life."

"When you say the motive's personal, though, you're forgetting how professional the murder looks. Even Russo thinks so. And you said it yourself: three neat holes in the chest. The ordinary person keeps shooting until the gun's empty, an then he's lucky if he scores twice—and at that it's usually one shot in the left thigh and one that just happens to sever an artery or something."

"1 can't argue with you there, Steve boy. And I did get it straight from the horse's mouth: Vennezio was shot by three bullets placed in an eight-inch circle. No wild shots, nothing in the room disturbed. No fuss, no flurry. The police reconsturction is the essence of simplicity. The murderer rang the bell. Dominic answered. Then he got shot. Then the murderer disappeared into the mists. One witness thought she heard the shots, and another witness thought he remembered seeing a car leave the community parking area about that time. But that's all."

"Could the witness identify the car?"

"Of course. It was a medium-size, dark sedan. Maybe a Ford, or possibly a Chevrolet. Or it could have been a Pontiac, he finally decided, or maybe a Mercury—or a Plymouth, or a Dodge."

"No license number."

"That's correct."

"Do the police think Vennezio was shot at the door, as soon as he answered it?"

"Now, that's a rather beguiling point. It seems that official opinion is divided on exactly where he stood when he got shot. The body actually lay, as I remember

119

it, with the feet toward the door and the head in a direct line away. In other words, he was lying as if he might have fallen directly on his back as he faced the door. However, the feet measured maybe ten or eleven feet from the door, and there was a certain amount of blood on the carpet between the feet and the door, indicating that he might possibly have been shot as he stood at the door, then staggered back, then got shot again and finally fell in the living room. Of course, there's also the possibility that he could have walked back into the room, then got shot."

"It makes a difference, though, which way you figure it. If he got shot at the door, the chances are that he didn't know the murderer—or at least didn't know him very well. If the shooting actually occurred while Vennezio was inside with the door closed behind him, that's a different matter."

"Very good." Dick nodded, burlesqueing a ponderous approval. "Very sound detection. I will only correct you on one point."

"What's that?"

"Well, it's already been established that Vennezio wasn't in the habit of unlocking the door at night until he looked through a peephole. So we can assume that he knew the murderer. We can also assume that the better they knew each other, the farther the murderer probably got inside before firing the fatal shot. As you said."

"I wish I could see the police photos," I mused.

"I can probably get copies for you. If not, we've got pictures in our files. I don't think they'll help much, though. There wasn't any sign of a struggle. Neither was there a package of Egyptian cigarettes on the coffee table,

120

nor a woman's embroidered handkerchief lying beneath the body."

"Do you know how many people were questioned?"

"As I remember it, I'd say most of your cast of characters was questioned, more or less perfunctorily. Russo made a state appearance at headquarters, flanked by two well-tailored lawyers. Sabella was there, too. It was all very convincing—and very brief."

"What about Mrs. Hanson?"

"She was questioned at the scene of the crime and then later at her place. I don't think she went down to headquarters."

"What about the anonymous phone tip?"

"That, too," Gross said, "is a rather beguiling point and one that you haven't stumbled across, apparently."

"How do you mean?"

"Well it seems that the police were tipped before Mrs. Hanson arrived on the scene. According to her story, she'd only been on the premises a few minutes when the police arrived."

I felt a quick lift of excitement as I asked, "What time did the phone call come in, do you know?"

"Just a few minutes before eight, if I'm not mistaken. And Mrs. Hanson said that she arrived about eight-fifteen. Is that what she told you?"

"Yes. That's exactly what she said."

"Do you believe her?"

I thought about it, finally saying, "Yes, I do. As nearly as I can see, she told me a completely straight story. She even seemed anxious to tell it all. Everything."

"Did she mention the anonymous phone call?"

"No," I admitted. "Not a word. But then I didn't ask.

Somehow it never occurred to me." I sat silently for a moment, thinking about it. "Did the police make any effort to find out who phoned?"

"Sure. But they didn't get very far. They questioned everyone who was living nearby or who might've been on the beach."

"I wonder," I said slowly, "whether it could've been the murderer who called."

Gross nodded, eyeing me ironically. "One wonders indeed. It's a pity your vision faded so soon." He smiled. "I still think that's a nice touch, that cloak."

"But why would he have called—and so soon? What time did the witness think she heard the shots?"

"Between seven thirty and eight. She wasn't sure."

I shook my head. "It's crazy."

"What's crazy?"

"That the murderer would call. It doesn't make sense."

"That's true, if you assume he called merely to lighten the policeman's burden. However, there's another explanation."

"What's that?"

"He might've known that Mrs. Hanson was due at the beachhouse."

"You mean he might've wanted to frame her for the murder?"

Gross spread his hands. "Can you think of a better reason? Nothing else makes much sense, that I can see."

"But there wasn't any other effort made to frame her. Nothing of hers was left at the scene of the crime." I paused. "Was there?"

"No. There were things of hers in the house, of course. But there wasn't any embroidered handkerchief under the body."

"What kind of a gun was used?"

"A .32," he answered, watching me. "What's known in the trade as a woman's gun. Unlike the more efficient .38 or .45, universally favored by cop and hood alike."

"All in an eight-inch circle, you said."

He nodded. "All in an eight-inch circle. Then he got in his car, drove to the nearest phone and called the police. Then he disappeared. Assuming, of course, that he was alone. We mustn't forget about the lady in the long cloak."

I shook my head. "That's hypothetical. It doesn't necessarily have any relation to what might've actually happened—or how it happened."

"What does it relate to?"

I snorted. "I've never known. And I've never said."

He looked at me for a long, silent moment. Then, thoughtfully, he said, "You know, I don't think you're really so different from any good, experienced cop who, after a few years on the force, can take one look at someone in the street and tell whether the guy's ever done time. The only real difference," he continued, "is in the effectiveness of your subconscious. Do you know what I mean?"

"Well, I—"

"You learn in Psychology 101," he continued, obviously warming to the subject, "that the subconscious is like a—a computer, filing a million punch cards of memories and impressions, only a very few of which register at any one time as conscious thought. In your case, though, I figure that you simply get a better alignment of cards than the rest of us. You don't necessarily have access to any more cards, it's just that the alignment is better. So, at some unpredictable moment, bingo: you've got the picture of the lady in her long flowing cloak."

"I guess that's probably true. I've never claimed that—"

"It could be that you've actually got a short circuit somewhere," he said, his familiar flippancy returning. "Did you ever think of that? It comes to you all at once, instead of gradually. The poor, plodding, underpaid, overworked cop trudges on and on, painfully gathering three facts a day, five days a week, until he's got fifteen: the magic number. You, on the other hand, plod on for the same five days, four of them big fat blanks. Then, on the fifth day, bingo: it all comes at once. The shock is such that you feel light-headed, naturally. You swoon. Then you call up headquarters, and then the *Sentinel*. Everyone thinks you're a phenomenon from the nether-world—completely forgetting the detective who's still out there somewhere in the night, racking up his three facts, then calling it a day—returning to a wife who's already been sound asleep on the sofa since halfway through the early late show."

I smiled, shrugged and spread my hands. "You've hit it, Dick. You've discovered my secret: a short circuit in the head. More coffee?"

"No, thanks."

"Doughnut?"

"No. I'd spoil my appetite for tuna salad." He looked at his watch, then began gathering up his cigarettes and matches. "What're you going to do?" he asked, toying with his hat.

"Just plod along, I guess, waiting for a short circuit."

"Are you still going with your mysterious couple on the beach?"

"According to what you've just said, I guess I should."

He nodded. "I think you should, too. However you do it, short circuit or not, you're a proven performer. From what you've told me, there're three women in Dominic Vennezio's life, either one of which could've got a mysterious male friend to do the job, for a cut of the swag."

"I'm not so sure Mrs. Hanson qualifies on that basis, especially if she has to cut up the swag. Ten thousand dollars isn't much money these days. Besides, she probably got that much from Dominic every six months—and had someone to keep her warm besides."

He rose to his feet, adjusting his hat.

"Maybe. Still, I wouldn't check off Mrs. Hanson just yet. Not until you're certain someone wasn't trying to frame her. That could be motive enough in itself, you know. Everyone isn't preoccupied with money. Take Russo, for instance. He could have done it for pure, red-blooded love—with a borrowed .32."

I reached in my pocket, searching for loose change. "I think you're reading too much into that .32, Dick. I've heard of hired professionals using .22's because of the noise. After all, it's a matter of accuracy. A .22 in the right spot can be deadlier than a .45."

"No argument. In fact, I can even top your own point. Two or three weeks ago a moderately successful pimp was murdered with one of these compressed-air pellet guns. He was playing poker, and no one knew he'd been shot till his head hit his chips."

"You're kidding."

"I'm not kidding. Those pellet guns're the newest

wrinkle in underworld armament. They're made in .22 caliber, as you know, and there's a new gun just on the market that's as powerful as a regular .22 rifle, at distances up to twenty feet. And, of course, there's the no-noise advantage."

"True." I left a tip, and we walked together to the door. "Say, will you do me a favor?"

"Why not?"

"See if you can find out what Larry Sabella said to the police when he was questioned. He had as much motive as anyone—more than most, when you think about it."

Gross smiled. "You mean when you double think about it. One time around, he's a lot better with Russo pulling the trigger." He opened the restaurant door, and we stepped out onto the sidewalk. "Nevertheless, I'll see what I can find out. Where're you staying?"

"The Prescott Motel."

"Okay. Thanks for the snack. If you don't get both legs broken, why don't you come out to the house for dinner tonight?"

"Thanks, Dick. But to be honest, I'd as soon get this business finished and get back to San Francisco. The longer I'm here, the jumpier I get."

"I see what you mean. All right, I'll be in touch."

"Thanks again." I stood for a moment watching him stride away. I was turning toward my car when I caught a brief glimpse of a familiar profile in the driver's seat of a white sedan parked halfway down the block. It was Carrigan. The large nose and protuberant eyes were unmistakable.

8

I LEFT Dick Gross about 4:30, got into my car and for the next fifteen minutes aimlessly drove, watching Carrigan's white sedan in the rear view mirror. He made no particular effort at concealment; he drove directly behind me rather than allow the usual one or two cars between. As I watched him, I became increasingly annoyed. He must know that his presence endangered me. Yet he obviously didn't care.

I noticed that the traffic was becoming much heavier as the rush hour approached. On an impulse I turned onto a convenient freeway, with no idea where it led. Quickly I accelerated, watching Carrigan follow, but now with a car between. I was in the right-hand lane; ahead was a turnoff. I waited until the last safe moment, then took the turnoff. As I swung into the cloverleaf, I could still see the white sedan in my mirror, two cars behind. I stayed on the cloverleaf, then cut in front of a furniture van. With the van shielding me, I turned back onto the freeway, going in the opposite direction. It worked. Smiling, I lit a cigarette and then settled back, switching on the radio. As I did, I noticed a Malibu sign. In all the years I'd lived in California, I'd never been to Malibu, just a few miles down the road. Now, I decided, was the time for a good seafood dinner, preceded by a martini, accompanied by a good bottle of wine and followed by cognac.

All during my excellent dinner the puzzle of Dominic Vennezio's murder ceaselessly revolved in my thoughts. Who would have murdered him, then called the police? Certainly no one in organized crime. Certainly no one hoping to gain directly by the murder. And how should I interpret my last night's vision? Who was the woman? What was her actual role in the ghostly tableau? Had she been a grim, silent witness—or a conspirator, directing the assassin?

Who was the woman? Charlene? Her mother? Mrs. Hanson? And what of the theory that the murderer had actually aimed the crime at Mrs. Hanson? According to that theory, Mrs. Hanson could have been the cloaked figure on the beach, but she might have been an unwilling spectator, tortured and tormented, responding to the murderer's diabolical whim.

Who, then, would have desired both the death of Dominic and the anguish of his mistress? Aidia Vennezio, my employer, was an obvious suspect. But there were others —Charlene, perhaps, aided by Larry Sabella, with his own compelling reasons. Russo could have done it—for love or for a different motive, secret still. But then came the matter of the phone call. If the murderer had indeed phoned, Sabella and Russo were eliminated. Because the murderer, according to Dick Gross's theory, was willing to gamble his life against Mrs. Hanson's—hoping to incriminate her. Who would have conceived such a gamble? The husband, John Hanson—a loser with nothing more to lose? Someone fanatically devoted to Aidia— Reggie Fay, perhaps? Angelo Vennezio might have done it, both to avenge his mother and to inherit a hundred thousand dollars.

Yet none of it seemed logical. The more I considered, the more I was inclined to doubt that the murderer had actually intended to incriminate Mrs. Hanson—or, at least, it seemed improbable that incriminating her was his primary purpose. Rather, the phone call might indicate the murderer's actual willingness to be captured—a death wish.

Who, then, could have been completely indifferent to his own fate, yet had hated Dominic Vennezio enough to kill him? Who could have known precisely when and where to strike—expertly, perhaps even professionally?

The more I thought about it, the more confusing the puzzle seemed. Logic had never been a specialty of mine. I could easily conceive the questions. But sorting them out and then arranging them into a coherent pattern had always been difficult for me.

So, over dessert, I turned my attention to the view out over the ocean—and to a statuesque blonde three tables away, dining with a repulsively fat little man wearing a nubby silk sports jacket, sunglasses and two large diamond rings.

By seven o'clock I'd finished my dinner and drinks. A little after seven thirty I was turning into Mrs. Hanson's block, parking across the street from the house and three doors down. Her house was darkened. I switched off the engine, rolled up the window and prepared to wait. I'd decided on a double martini before dinner and a double cognac later—and I'd had a split of white wine with the dinner, instead of just a glass. I was feeling drowsy and was surrendering to the luxury of allowing my eyes to close when a car turned the corner and came toward me. As I watched, the car pulled to the curb in front of the Hanson house. I turned in my seat for a better view. I could see two figures inside the car: a woman on the passenger's side and a man driving. They seemed to be talking together. Then the passenger's door opened. The woman got out, nodded to the driver and began walking slowly to the front door, fumbling in her handbag, head bent. The car began pulling away. As it gathered speed, I realized that the car was a Buick—a new Buick sedan.

Mr. Russo gets two new Buicks a year, Montez had said.

Quickly I looked again, trying to make out the license number. But at that moment the car turned a nearby corner.

How many Buick sedans were registered in Los Angeles County? Two thousand? More?

I got out of the car, locked it and breathed deeply as I walked toward Mrs. Hanson's door. The air in La Palada was better than that in Los Angeles. I wondered whether the Outfit had considered the smog situation in selecting its own private town.

I rang the bell, and as I waited I belatedly realized that I had no clear plan. But more and more it seemed Mrs. Hanson had been involved, either as a focus for revenge or because of her relationship to either Vennezio or Russo, possibly both. She . . .

130

The door came open. She was wearing a tailored suit and house slippers. As she recognized me her eyebrows arched in surprise. Involuntarily, she stepped back a single quick pace, her hand moving to the door as if to close it.

"I know I should've phoned," I said. "But I just got back in town. If you could spare a few minutes . . ." I let the sentence go unfinished. For the second time that day I realized how an unwelcome salesman must feel, standing hat in hand, smiling with stiff lips.

She looked at me, unsmiling. Then, without speaking, she turned back into the house, walking directly into the living room. I closed the door and followed her.

How should I begin? Should I ask her about the Buick? I decided against it. Better to find some neutral ground.

She switched on a lamp and sat on the sofa, motioning for me to sit opposite her, as we'd sat the day before.

"I hope you've eaten," I began. "As I drove up, I saw that you were just coming in. I wouldn't want to—"

"I ate after work," she answered, staring at me with her calm gray eyes.

"Oh. Good." I nodded, smiled and cleared my throat. "Since I saw you yesterday," I said, "I've learned a couple of things that I don't think you know, concerning Dominic Vennezio's murder. For instance, I looked into the actual time element of the murder. I discovered that the murder probably occurred not more than a half hour before you arrived at the beachhouse."

"I told you that yesterday," she said tonelessly.

"I know. But what you didn't tell me—or at least what we didn't discuss—is that the police were notified

131

sometime during that half hour."

She didn't reply.

"Do you have any idea who might've phoned the police, Mrs. Hanson?"

"N—no. How could I?"

"Do you know who the police think phoned them?"

She didn't reply, simply staring. She sighed once, deeply.

"They think it was the murderer."

"The—the murderer? But—"

"But what, Mrs. Hanson?"

"But that doesn't seem—I mean . . ." She made a small, helpless gesture, resigned.

"It doesn't seem logical. Is that what you were going to say?"

"Yes, I—I suppose it was."

"I thought the same thing myself. But then it occurred to me that the murderer might've known you were on your way to the beachhouse. He might've wanted the police to arrive just after you."

"But why should—I mean—"

"The murderer might've wanted to see you blamed for the murder, Mrs. Hanson."

Suddenly she twisted in a swift movement of protest, her body now tensed "No—no. It couldn't've been that."

"Why do you say that?"

"Well, I . . ." She seemed puzzled, then her body again went slack. "I don't know," she said dully. "But I— I just——"

"The last time we talked, we discussed what might've happened if the murderer had arrived a little later—or

132

you'd arrived a little earlier. The idea that you could've been on the scene—perhaps even murdered—didn't seem to disturb you. Yet, now, you can't believe that the murderer might've wanted to see you framed. You seemed disturbed at the thought. Why?"

"I told you yesterday that the thought of being dead no longer terrifies me, Mr. Drake. Maybe that's your answer."

I slowly nodded, watching her as she sat with head slightly bowed, staring down at the floor.

"I learned something else, Mrs. Hanson," I said. "Something that also concerns you directly."

With an obvious effort she raised her head, meeting my eyes. "I'm very tired tonight, Mr. Drake," she said. "Whatever it is, I—I wish you'd tell me quickly."

"Yes, certainly," I answered almost solicitously—then immediately felt irked at the sympathy I felt. For a moment I looked away from her drawn face. Then, doggedly, I got on with it: "You told me last night," I began, "that you had no idea why your husband left you. Is that right?"

She nodded, silently.

I took a deep breath, then said, "I discovered today, Mrs. Hanson, that Dominic Vennezio forced your husband to go away."

To my surprise, she only smiled: a brief, bitter twisting of the mouth.

"I've heard that before. I even asked Dominic about it."

"Did he deny it?"

She nodded.

"Did he also deny that he offered your husband ten thousand dollars to go away, provided he'd never come back?"

"Ten thou—"

"And as far as I know," I continued, "your husband agreed. Of course," I added, "I also understand that your husband really had no choice. He probably would've been forced to leave, with or without the money. But the fact remains that—"

"He—he was paid to go? He took money, and left?" She seemed unable to grasp it.

"That's what I understand, Mrs. Hanson. I've no proof, of course, but . . ."

I realized that she was crying, soundlessly. Slowly her head dropped down, and her shoulders began to shake. She raised her hands to her face, palms pressed flat against her cheeks. Her fingers, I saw, were wet with her tears.

"I'm sorry, Mrs. Hanson. Really. I—I hope you don't think that . . ." I got to my feet and fumbled in my jacket for a clean handkerchief. "Here." I dropped the handkerchief in her lap. "Here. Take this."

"Th—thank you." She blew her nose and wiped at her eyes.

"I'm sorry," I said again.

"It . . ." She swallowed, sniffed and once more pressed the handkerchief to her nose. "It's all right. You—you're really a very kind man, Mr. Drake. I—I don't understand how you . . ." She let the thought go unfinished. I knew what she meant to say. She didn't understand how I could be working for the Outfit.

"I'll be going now, Mrs. Hanson. I'd just like to ask you

one more—"

"He always did everything wrong," she said, her voice thick and muffled. "Always. If he'd just told me. Or if he'd just—just stayed, and faced it. He—I—" She shook her head.

"Have you ever had two or three men pound you in the face with their fists, Mrs. Hanson—and then prop you against the side of a building when you start to fall, so they can make sure your nose is broken—and then finally let you fall, so they can start kicking you?"

She raised her head, looking at me mutely.

"It happened to me once," I said. "I didn't know it was coming. I hadn't been warned, as they probably warned your husband. But I'll tell you this: I'd've done anything to get out of that beating. It was the worst experience of my life. I'll never forget it." As I spoke, I was thinking of Larry Sabella's threat. For the first time, vividly, I imagined the pain, having both legs broken.

She rose and for a moment stood before me, her head bowed.

"It was all my fault," she said finally. "Everything that happened to John, it was my fault. I'm—I'm just like my mother. Exactly."

She turned and walked past me, toward the front door. "I'm sorry, Mr. Drake," she said indistinctly. "I don't know why I should be shocked that John would leave me for ten thousand dollars. I guess it's just that it—it makes the whole mess complete. Everyone's for sale. For a few thousand dollars, you can find someone who'll do anything—anything at all. So now it—it's complete. Everything. Everything's gone. Completely gone." She stood in the small entryway, leaning against the paneled wall,

135

head bowed. Waiting for me to leave.

"You've got your son, though," I said.

"No, Mr. Drake. I *had* my son. Years ago. A long, long time ago."

I reached for the doorknob, turned it and slowly opened the door. The night air felt very fresh. La Palada air. Private property.

On the porch I turned, ready to try the question I'd come to ask her.

"Do you know," I began slowly, "whether Dominic Vennezio thought he had any reason to be—jealous of you? Or rather, jealous of . . ." I cleared my throat. "Jealous of another man?"

Slowly she raised her head. Her voice was tight with a kind of despairing fury as she whispered:

"I was only a gangster's mistress, Mr. Drake. I wasn't a gangster's whore."

She closed the door, very softly. Behind the door, I heard her sobbing.

Dejectedly I made my way down her flagstone walk, pausing at the sidewalk to light a cigarette.

Had I discovered anything? Had I accomplished anything, aside from torturing her? She'd seemed shocked that the murderer might have wanted her caught at the murder scene. Did she, then, suspect the murderer's identity?

Who, of all the possible suspects, would be closest to her, therefore accounting for her shocked response? Obviously, her anonymous lover—if he really existed. Or possibly her husband.

Did she suspect someone? Was there really a lover? Suddenly I realized that I must follow her, day and night, until I discovered the answer. And, having made the decision, I remembered Dick Gross's image of the poor, plodding cop, collecting his three facts a day, five days a week. A few hours ago, the image had seemed funny. Now, I merely sighed. I was probably about to begin a long, tedious exercise in utter futility.

Slowly I crossed the street, heading for my car. The night was pleasant and warm; my footfalls had a reassuring, small-town cadence in the quiet darkness. I paused at the car, searching for my keys while I stared across at the Hanson house. Had it been only yesterday that I'd first talked to her? It seemed . . .

Close by shrubbery rustled. Suddenly I was whirling from the sound, instinctively throwing myself aside. Yet my movements felt so terribly slow. Dim light glinted on the dark gun barrel, following me. The single instant of blind, helpless panic congealed my thoughts into a frozen kaleidoscope of helpless terror. I was in Korea. I was unarmed. Defenseless. *Zigzag*, they'd taught us. *Hit the dirt.* I saw the shrubbery rustle sharply with the muzzle blast. Clearly I could see the gun barrel—a thick, heavy barrel. My shoulder struck the sidewalk; I was rolling toward the car—the front of the car. In Korea I'd once rolled under a truck, clanging my helmet on the drive shaft, hearing the shrill, savage whine of the sniper's bullets, ricocheting close beside me. Would the next shot . . . ?

Shot.

It was all silent. Everything. The night was soundless. My shoulder was wedged between the front bumper and the pavement. I had trapped myself.

I was on my feet, sobbing for breath as I sprinted, zigzagging across the street. Ahead was the Hanson front yard, closer now. I tripped on the curb, wildly recovered and threw myself toward the base of a nearby palm tree. Panting heavily, I scambled behind the trunk, stretching full on the ground, searching the darkness. If he came for me, I would run back deeper into the shadows.

But nothing stirred. The shrubbery across the street was faintly illuminated by a nearby street light, and nothing stirred.

I was beginning to tremble violently. Slowly, I rested my head against the palm tree. As I did, I was aware that I was moving my hand up to my head, as if to adjust a steel helmet.

9

I was hardly aware of having driven from the Hanson house to the Prescott Motel. I remembered switching off the engine and headlights. Now I was sitting motionless behind the wheel, unable to move.

Had I imagined it? Could it possibly have been a boy, playing? There'd been no sound of a shot. In the uncertain light, I could have imagined the muzzle blast rippling the foliage.

It might have been a prank.

Or he might have used a silencer. Or, according to Dick Gross, a pellet gun. Had there been a ricochet? I couldn't remember. The endless moments I'd spent wedged beneath the car's front end had been wildly confused with the memory of Korea, pinned down under the truck, hearing the ricochet of the sniper's bullets. I remembered that I'd soiled myself as I'd crouched beneath the truck. Crouched behind Mrs. Hanson's palm tree, I'd merely trembled. For what seemed like hours, I'd trembled. Then, incredibly, I'd begun to feel foolish. A teenage couple had strolled by within a few feet of me, their arms intertwined, laughing softly together. Somehow they'd given me a sheepish courage, and when I saw a man leisurely strolling on the opposite side of the street I'd gotten covertly to my feet, brushed at my clothing and quickly crossed to my car. It had seemed as if the engine would never start, but finally I pulled away, aware that the strolling man was looking at me with open curiosity.

Now, stiffly climbing from the car and crossing the brightly lit motel parking lot, the incident seemed vague and remote. Dispassionately, I recognized that I was in mild shock. It was an advantage of having experienced combat; I knew what to expect. I knew that I would probably sleep very soundly that night and awake to a heightened awareness of sound, color and sensation. It was nature's way, a sergeant used to say. But he would never explain.

I let myself into my room from the parking lot. I locked and bolted the door, drew the blinds and then switched on the lights. I poured a half-glass of bourbon and drank of it while I lifted the phone, got the desk and asked for Carrigan. I was told that he'd checked out earlier in the day. Too exhausted to decide whether I felt relieved or disappointed, I undressed and fell into bed in my underwear, having refilled my glass. I lay propped on the pillows, drinking—feeling the liquor's languor flow first through my limbs, then through my consciousness. This, I was thinking, was how John Hanson must feel, drifting away from reality. This was the sensation the alcoholic craved—this sad, sodden surcease from the self.

What could I do? For eight thousand dollars, what could I do? I'd already decided to follow Mrs. Hanson, hour by hour, day by day, until I discovered whether her lover really existed.

Would I do it?

Would the man with the strange, silent weapon try again? Would he succeed, next time?

Somehow, it didn't seem to matter. As I drained the glass and switched off the light, I realized that it seemed very important to live tomorrow exactly as I'd planned it: following Faith Hanson minute by minute, hour by hour. As I closed my eyes, I vaguely wondered why.

Two days later, at about 8:30 on Wednesday night, I was parked within a few hundred feet of the spot where I'd run so wildly from the sight of the silent gun barrel. I'd been following Faith Hanson steadily for two days, uneventfully. Now, from the safety of my car, I was staring fixedly at the shrubbery, remembering. The gesture seemed a kind of timid defiance; I felt like a small boy, taunting the neighborhood bully from the security of my front porch. Yet, returning, I felt braver—better. It was another lesson I'd learned in Korea: everything has its limit, even fear. Courage, for some, is simply a surfeit of fear—a final, desperate alternative to the self revealed a coward.

So, idly, I switched on the car radio, searching for a news broadcast. I was yawning as I twirled the dial, thinking that, next day, I should buy a Thermos bottle for coffee.

Then, as I was wondering how much a good Thermos would cost, I became aware of a disembodied sense of diffused reality—a strange sensation of time and place suspended. Slowly I raised my eyes, searching for the focus of the feeling.

141

I saw the figure of a man slowly walking down the sidewalk in the direction of the Hanson house. His silhouette was stooped and defeated, his steps shuffling and uncertain.

I was parked across the street; he was perhaps six doors down from the house when I first saw him. I blinked, striving for a sharper vision through the obscure aura of recognition and recall.

Without conscious decision, I'd switched off the radio, opened the car door and was walking across the street. He was coming from the opposite direction; the Hanson house was almost exactly midway between us. I stopped beneath the dark shadows of a tree, waiting. How often had he come, in the past weeks?

What would he do?

What had he done?

He was standing in front of the house, staring uncertainly. He ventured a hesitant step up the flagstones, toward the carved front door. But now he paused, stopped and finally retreated. Then, defeated, he turned away—walking back in the direction from which he'd come.

I overtook him within a block. He seemed unaware of my presence as I fell into step beside him.

"Are you Mr. Hanson?" I asked quietly. "John Hanson?"

For a moment he didn't respond. Then, slowly, he turned his head. He was about my height, and thin. He wore a shapeless windbreaker; his blond hair was matted and unkempt. In the dim light of the streetlamps I recognized the lifeless, opaque eyes of the drunk. Beneath the stained stubble of a week's beard his face was deeply, despairingly creased into lines of ravaged despondency.

He looked at me, rapidly blinking. Then, still shuffling along, he turned away without having spoken.

Ahead was a neighborhood bar. It was still early on a week night; the place would probably be almost deserted.

"I'd like to talk to you, Mr. Hanson." I pointed to the bar. "Can we go in there? Maybe you'd . . ." I hesitated, soothing my conscience with the rationalization that now one drink more or less wouldn't matter. "Maybe you'd like something to drink."

Once more the lifeless eyes turned to me. Then, an expression of vague amusement flickered feebly.

"How much information do you want—for how many drinks?"

Not replying, I guided him into the bar. We slid into a booth, sitting on red plastic benches, facing each other across a red Formica tabletop.

Hanson ordered a double shot of bourbon; I ordered bourbon and water. Until the drinks came, we sat silently, avoiding one another's eyes. I didn't know what Hanson was feeling, and I was almost unwilling to begin my probing. Finally, though, after a long gulp of my highball, I said:

"I've talked to both Mrs. Hanson and Johnny during the past few days, Mr. Hanson. I—I'm trying to find out who murdered Dominic Vennezio."

He didn't reply, but sat perfectly motionless, staring at the glass of whisky on the table before him. His hands rested inertly on either side of the glass. Then, in a low, distant voice, he said, "Different things make you realize what's happened to you. A long time ago, whisky was my problem. Now it's wine. I haven't had a drink of whisky

143

in months—it's been that long since someone bought me a drink. If you get money, you see, you buy wine. Not whisky. So . . ." He raised an unsteady hand, gesturing toward the glass. "So, when I see a glass of whisky and know it's mine, I—I" He shook his head. Then, sighing deeply, he took up the glass, lifting it slowly to his lips. He sipped the dark liquid, grimaced and lowered the glass. "It's a—a defeat, in a way, drinking whisky. The last defeat."

I'd dealt with enough alcoholics to realize the futility of discussing their problems. They inevitably began by soddenly agreeing with you, then finished by cursing you.

So, quietly, I said, "Would you mind telling me what you've done during the past two years, Mr. Hanson? Since you left La Palada?"

He didn't answer, staring down into his glass. Then, slowly and deliberately, he pushed the glass away from him, until it rested at a midpoint between us. His hands, I saw, were red and cracked, with many white scars and running sores. His fingernails were dirty and broken.

With his hands flat on the table, he raised his head, meeting my eyes. In the movement, with the hands stretched out before him, there was a sense of supplication. Yet his eyes were steady, searching my own, intently.

"Who are you?"

"My name is Drake. Stephen Drake."

"You've seen Faith, you say."

"Yes. I've been hired to find out who murdered Dominic Vennezio. As I told you."

"And have you found out, Mr. Drake?" As he asked the

question, quietly and rationally, I realized that he wasn't actually drunk—not now. I realized, too, that his mind was more alert than his dispirited, humiliated bearing made it seem. As Russo would have said, class tells. They'd driven a sports car, Mrs. Hanson had said, and hired caterers for their cocktail parties.

"No, I haven't found out," I replied. "I'm still trying, though."

"Do you think Faith had something to do with the murder?"

"I don't know. I think, though, that somehow she might have been a reason for the murder, without being actually involved."

"A reason." He nodded. "Yes, I see what you mean. Faith has been a reason for lots of things. Take me, for instance."

"I know. She told me."

"Did she?" Sadly he smiled. "Perhaps she's repenting. It could happen, I suppose."

"Does she know you're in town?"

"No."

"Have you lived here in Los Angeles for the whole two years, Mr. Hanson?"

"No. When I left, I went back to San Francisco—home. I stayed there for a year and a half."

"You've been back here for about six months, then."

"Yes."

"What have you been doing, for those six months?"

He raised his right hand, turning it for my inspection.

"I've been washing dishes, Mr. Drake. It's a trade I learned in San Francisco, after my money ran out. Have you found out about my money?"

145

"The ten thousand dollars, you mean?"

He nodded. "Yes, the ten thousand dollars."

I nodded in return. "Yes, I know about that."

"Does Faith know?"

"Yes, she does."

"Did you tell her?"

I sighed, deeply. "Yes, I did. I—I'm sorry."

For a long moment he looked at me. Then, wearily, he smiled. With his red, sore-splotched hand he scratched at his stubble. "You're honest—an honest man."

"Thank you."

"Do you work for Frank Russo?"

"No." I finished my drink. Silently he watched me, then pointed to the glass resting midway between us.

"Take mine. My doctors say I shouldn't drink." Ironically he accented the phrase.

I did as he asked.

"Wasn't it dangerous for you," I said, "coming back to Los Angeles while Vennezio was still alive?"

"It might've been. I didn't care. I came to see my son."

"Your son? But—"

"But what, Mr. Drake?"

"He said he hadn't—I mean—"

"Did he say he hadn't seen me?"

"Well, yes. He said that—"

"He's probably trying to forget it. You see, when I first got to town I used to follow Faith, at a distance. I didn't care about her; I was looking for Johnny. I discovered, after several weeks, that he came home every second or third weekend. Gradually, I learned his habits. He'd often go to a movie on Sunday afternoons, and when I could afford it I'd go to the same movie and sit where I could see him. I used to save my money, so I could go to the movies."

I didn't reply. There was nothing I could say.

"Then, one day," he continued, "he saw me. I was sitting five or six rows behind him. He was going to the lobby for some popcorn, and he saw me."

"Wh—" I swallowed. "What happened, when he saw you?"

"He just stood in the aisle, staring at me. Finally the usher asked him to move, and he went out into the lobby. I—I followed him. It was all I could do. We—we went outside, to a park. We sat and talked for a few minutes —just a few minutes. And then . . ." He began to slowly shake his head. I saw that tears were streaking his grimy face. "And then, suddenly, Johnny was running away. He—he just got up from the bench and started to run. And—and—" He couldn't finish it. Still shaking his head, he began numbly to leave the garish red plastic booth. I gripped his arm.

"Have you ever been to the beach cabin, where Vennezio was murdered?" I asked. "Did you ever follow your wife there?"

He stared down at my hand on his arm and then slowly raised his gaze.

"Yes," he answered, "I followed her. once. Just once. A long time ago."

"How long?"

"Too long, for your purposes, Mr. Drake. It wasn't me who killed him. I would have done it. I thought about killing him every day of my life, for two years, now. When I heard he'd been murdered, I felt as if my last excuse for living had been taken from me. I—I used to

147

dream about killing him. I used to have hallucinations. It was always the same. There'd always be the three of us—Vennezio, Faith and me. She'd always be watching me when I killed him. And sometimes, when I'd have enough to drink, I was sure I could do it. But then, the next drink, I'd realize that I couldn't. I—I used to cry about it. I used to cry myself to sleep. Because, you see, it was all I had left—the last, pitiful illusion that somewhere, somehow, I could kill him."

Weakly, he tugged his arm until I released him.

I watched him shuffling out of the bar. From the back, he looked like any other drunk, wandering off into oblivion, alone.

It was always the same, he'd said. *There'd always be the three of us.*

Was it possible? Had his delusion somehow communicated itself to me? Could he have been nearby, last Sunday night?

Pulling into my motel parking space, I locked the car and walked to my room. It was almost 11 P.M., and I felt tired and depressed. I couldn't escape the gathering conviction that, somehow, John Hanson's delusion of murder had found its way into my own consciousness. Mental telepathy, after all, was virtually a recognized fact, as the Duke University experiments had proven, at least statistically.

I was fitting my key into the door when I heard a soft footstep behind me. Startled, I straightened and turned. Jimmy Montez stood in the darkness. He seemed to be smiling, standing graceful and relaxed—immaculate in sports jacket and slacks.

148

"H—hello," I said, retreating a step.

"Hi." In the single, softly spoken monosyllable I sensed a tension—and danger. The dim light of the parking lot revealed his eyes, watchful and darkly opaque—in hard, puposeful contrast to the lips still twisted in a small, mocking smile. He came forward. "We been waiting for you."

We stood perhaps three feet apart. Behind me was a flower bed; the calves of my legs were pressed against the low concrete wall surrounding the flowers.

"Waiting?" I looked around me. Across the parking lot, a man and a woman were walking away from their car chatting and laughing. I realized that my knees were beginning to tremble. Should I run? Shout for help? Should I try to . . .

"Mr. Russo wants to talk to you."

"Talk to me? But I . . ."

Montez raised his right hand, pointing. Following his gesture I saw the Buick. Dimly in the back seat I could see the figure of a man.

"Over there," he said.

"But . . ." Involuntarily, I was moving along the low concrete wall, away from him.

Now his left hand went to his jacket pocket. It was a slow, leisurely movement. Then, just as leisurely, the hand came out. I heard a small, sharp click. Looking down, I saw the bright sliver of a knife blade gleaming in the darkness.

"Over there," he repeated. "Walk."

"But——"

"Walk." With his right hand he gripped my left elbow, turning me toward the waiting car. He placed the

149

knife blade flat against my left arm. I was walking with him, powerless to resist. Dimly I wondered whether my legs would fail. I found myself thinking of Larson, shaking his head, calling me a fool—predicting that I'd find myself lying face down in the back seat of Russo's car, going for a ride.

I was standing beside the car now—the Buick. Larsen had called it a Cadillac. He'd been wrong, then. Wildly now, yet helplessly, my incoherent thoughts became entangled in the single, nonsensical refrain: he'd been wrong about the car, he could be wrong about the rest. He'd been wrong—wrong about the car. And maybe about the rest.

My knees were shaking violently.

Montez opened the door with his left hand. I wondered what he'd done with the knife.

"Get in."

I was sitting in the back seat, twisted to face Frank Russo. He was dressed in a dark business suit and wore a dark hat. He motioned for Montez to move away from the car.

"I'll make it short and sweet, Drake."

"But I—you—"

"I told you," he cut in, "that you weren't supposed to get any ideas of your own, about talking to the cops."

"But I—you're wrong. I—he—"

"You been talking to the CIIB." He paused. Then, quietly, he said, "Right?"

"Yes, but it—it wasn't my idea. I told him to go away. I—I—"

"That's not the point, Drake. The point is, you was supposed to tell me, whenever you talked to a cop.

150

Right?"

"Yes, but I—I was afraid that—"

"You was afraid I wouldn't like it. Is that it?"

"Yes. I—"

"You forgot that I'd like it even less, you talking to the cops, and not telling me."

"Yes. I see. I'm—I'm sorry. It—"

"It won't happen again. Is that what you was going to say?"

"Yes. I told him, the first time I talked to him, that he should—"

"All right, Drake." His voice sounded almost bored. "Let's forget about that cop. He could be back in Sacramento, for all I know."

"Well, yes he could. I know that he checked—"

"What else've you found out?"

"Wh—what else?"

Burlesqueing an elaborate patience, he nodded. "Right. What else. Anything you found out, you were supposed to let me know. Remember?"

"Well, yes. But I—I haven't—"

"What did you do Monday, for instance? Who'd you talk to?"

"Well, I—I went to Charlene Vennezio's, first. And I—I talked to her, for a while."

"What about?"

I decided to tell him the whole interview in detail, hopefully to wear down his patience. Instead, he became intently interested, and, too late, I realized that if he were really Faith Hanson's secret lover, Charlene's speculations about Faith's mysterious role in the murder would be an actual threat to Russo. I was becoming hopelessly

151

confused—unable to think fast enough to keep ahead of my story. And surely my confusion and fear must be perfectly plain to Russo, now watching me so closely.

I'll break both your legs, Larry Sabella had said. The threat echoed and reechoed with a desperate, hysterical clarity. Yet, still, I heard myself talking.

When I'd finished, Russo sat for a moment without speaking. Then he said, "What happened then—after you talked to Charlene?" He was watching me very carefully.

The moment had come. If I admitted talking to Sabella, I'd have to tell Russo everything. If I didn't admit talking to Sabella and Russo knew . . .

"What happened then, Drake?" His voice had become very quiet. And in that moment, looking at him, I decided I had no choice—no choice, and only one chance: that Russo hadn't yet learned of my conversation with Johnny Hanson. If I weren't questioned about that conversation, I could yet escape admitting to Russo that Sabella had named him as the same man Johnny Hanson had accused of murder.

"Well," I began, licking my lips, "after I talked to Charlene, I—I talked to Larry Sabella. He just happened to come by, I think. And we—he and I—we talked. He wanted to know what I'd found out, and—" I stopped talking. Too late.

"And you told him." I couldn't see his eyes; I couldn't assess his expression. But the cold, suppressed fury in the voice was unmistakable.

"But there wasn't anything to tell him. I—I hadn't found out anything, really. Nothing that's important. I still haven't. I just . . ."

"I'm going to ask you this just once, Drake. I'm going to ask you to tell me every word you told Sabella. Every single word. I'm not going to threaten you, like Sabella probably did. That's for punks—punks like Sabella. I'm just asking you—for your own good."

I opened my mouth, but couldn't speak. Suddenly I seemed to see myself from a point outside—moving my mouth soundlessly, too terrified to from a single word. I realized that, irrationally, I was reliving the exact moment last Saturday when I'd decided to return Mrs. Vennezio's check. I couldn't seem to think of anything but that single moment. I'd been in my apartment. In San Francisco. And I'd . . .

Russo was turning his head toward Montez, standing in the nearby shadows. Montez was lounging against the trunk of a huge palm tree, watching us.

Slowly, Russo was raising his hand, beginning a gesture to the waiting Montez.

I hardly realized that I was speaking. I remember that I was forced to gulp often for breath—deep, desperate gasps.

I'll break your legs, if you tell Russo. I'll break both your legs.

How had they threatened John Hanson? I'd never asked. He'd been drunk. Weak. I'd watched him shuffle off, pitying him for his weakness. Yet now I couldn't get my breath fast enough to keep up with the terrified rush of my own desperate confession.

I'd finished speaking. I realized that Russo was silent. I blinked, then turned toward him. His face was obscured in shadows.

"I made a mistake," he said finally. "Two mistakes.

153

First, I should've sent you back to San Francisco. I figured, though, that one man, working alone, couldn't find out anything. I was right, too. You haven't found out anything—not about the murder. But . . ." His voice trailed off. Then, in a more thoughtful cadence, he said, "My second mistake was Faith Hanson. What the hell I was thinking about, I'll never figure out. I still can't figure it out. But I know how Sabella is figuring—him and some back East." He paused, then shook his head, incredulous at his own thoughts—disgusted with himself.

"I told you, Drake," he said, "that you weren't cut out for this kind of thing. You just aren't tough enough. I was right—I always knew I was right. But I figured it'd be your problem, not mine."

"It—it is my problem, though. Sabella said—"

"I know what Sabella said," he snapped. "But if you'd've had any brains, you'd've walked out of that apartment and called me. I told you the first hour you were in town what to do. And I figured you got it. I figured you were smart. Not tough, maybe. But at least smart."

"But it—it wasn't a matter of brains. It—it's just that I was frightened. Scared."

Suddenly he snorted, then actually laughed. He took off his hat, tapped it on the seat front before him, then threw it irritably at the steering wheel. He shook his head.

"You're something, Drake. You're really something else. That I gotta admit." He drew a hand across his balding pate and again shook his head. "The funny thing is, I still like you." He turned to look at me fully. "And I guess that I can thank you, in a way. At least now I know what

154

Sabella is up to. That's something."

I couldn't think of a reply. I could only think that now he wouldn't kill me. I knew it. Hesitantly, then, I began telling him about the attack on me, Monday night. I knew now that Russo hadn't ordered the attack. Therefore, if he felt that Syndicate discipline had been violated, Russo might protect me from another attempt.

When I'd finished, he sat silently for a moment, thoughtfully frowning. Finally he said, "How come you didn't tell me this before?"

"Well, I guess I—I was afraid to talk to you after everything Sabella said. I guess I just . . ." I shrugged.

"Sabella." He pronounced it as if the name were an obscenity. Then slowly he asked, "Do you figure that I killed Vennezio?" He was watching me closely.

I shook my head.

"Why don't you?"

"Because it—it— wouldn't've been—smart."

He smiled, now a little wearily. "That's right. That's the right answer, Drake. It wouldn't've been smart. You've got it just right. I was stupid once, falling for Faith. I—I never thought anything like that could happen to me, as old as I am. When I was twenty, yes. But now—" He shook his head.

"Have you—are you deeply involved with her? Still?"

"Not now," he said. "Not since Dom died. I just—just couldn't afford to see her. And the funny thing is, I only talked to her four or five times, before Dom got knocked off. That's all, just four or five times. And we just talked, nothing else. It's . . ." Baffled, he bunched a fist, lightly pounding his knee. "It's the craziest thing—I never heard of anything so crazy—let alone thinking it could happen

155

to me. It all started when I first got out here. Dom was already in hot water because of her. And those damn letters of Aidia's, they might've been trouble for everyone. So I went to see Faith, to tell her to get out of town—or at least to break it off with Dom. I'd already talked to Dom, but he was stubborn. He said that Faith was all that meant anything to him. He was in love." Russo snorted, spreading his hands. "I laughed at him. Then, before I knew what'd happened, I found myself seeing her again—to talk things over with her. And then—" He shrugged.

"The plain truth is," he said slowly, "that if they thought, back East, that I'd killed Vennezio because of a woman, I'd probably get exactly what Dom got. And quick."

I didn't reply. Strangely, I felt sorry for him. Watching him, I thought he seemed tired—possibly frightened.

"What've you been doing since Monday?" he asked, with an obvious effort at getting down to business.

"I've been following Mrs. Hanson."

"Why?"

"I was trying to find out about the—the man in her life. I didn't really think it was you. But I thought that maybe Johnny Hanson might really know something. Anyhow, it was all I had to go on."

"You don't have any idea who killed him, then?"

I shook my head.

"This kid—Faith's kid. Why d'you suppose he said what he did?"

"I don't know."

"Do you think he saw something the night Dom got killed?"

"No. He said he'd never been to the beachhouse. I've been thinking that, whatever he knew, he must've found out from his mother."

Russo glanced at me sharply.

"He told you he'd never been out to the beachhouse?"

I nodded.

"That's a bunch of crap," he said abruptly. "I saw him there myself, once. Isn't he a blond kid, that drives a Mustang?"

"Yes."

"Well, then, he's lying. I—" He hesitated. "I went out there myself, once." He ruefully smiled. "I remember thinking that I was acting like a—a kid myself, mooning around. Anyhow, I saw this kid, parked in the parking area. I'd only seen him once before, but I'm pretty sure it was him."

"Do you think he saw you?"

Decisively he shook his head. "No chance. None at all."

"And you're reasonably certain it was Johnny Hanson you saw?"

He shrugged. "I'm not positive, but . . ." His voice trailed off, and for a long moment he stared away, thinking. Then he said, "As long as you're mixed up in this, Drake, I'll tell you how it is, as far as I'm concerned." Again he paused, thinking. Then, in a more decisive voice he said, "The only thing that's going to help me now is for you—or someone—to find out who killed Dom. I don't know how busy Sabella has been, back East. I don't know how far he's got, with his little plan. I'll have to check, and that'll take a little time. In the meantime, though, you'd better get working—and hard. What about these—these voices of yours, or whatever they are? Is that just a bunch of bull, or what?"

I told him about the single vision I'd had.

"Hell, that could mean anything," he answered irritably. "Anything at all. Is that how you got this big reputation of yours? With daydreams like that?"

"Well, I—"

"I'll tell you how it looks to me, Drake," he said suddenly. "If there's anything to that—that daydream of yours, I figure the woman is Charlene, and the triggerman is Sabella. She said it herself: Dom dies, and she inherits a bundle of money, plus Sabella gets a shot at the swivel chair. Maybe it didn't look like that to you at first. I mean, it didn't make sense for Sabella to kill a guy who was already out of a job. But if Sabella can make it look like I murdered Dom because of Faith, then—" He didn't bother to finish it.

I was shaking my head. "But I can't—I mean—"

"You can't what?"

"Well, if Sabella is the one, I—I—"

"Listen, Drake. About the only chance you've got to keep yourself in one piece is to prove that it *is* Sabella. If he's the guy, I'll take care of it. You won't have to worry about what he'll do to you when he finds out you been talking to me. If it isn't him . . ." He shook his head. "If it isn't, there isn't much I can do for you. I'll sooner or later take care of Sabella, one way or the other—to get myself off the hook. But I'm sure not going to put myself in the soup for you—especially after you were so goddam stupid."

"But—"

"But nothing." He reached across and opened the door

on my side. His expression was calmly, brutally decisive. His voice was dead level. "You'd better get yourself some sleep, Drake. And you'd better get yourself some results. Because when Sabella finds out you been talking to me, he's going to start wondering—and he's probably going to want to talk with you. See what I mean?"

"But—"

"If I was you, I'd talk to that Hanson kid. Like we say in the movies, he knows more than he's telling."

He pushed the door wider, at the same time signaling for Montez.

Hastily I got out of the car, and with my first step almost stumbled and fell. Recovering myself, I watched the big Buick pull out of the parking lot.

I was completely drained—even of fear. As I fitted my key into the door, a hackneyed refrain from countless scenarios tumbled through my thoughts: *I'll never get out alive, I'll never get out alive.*

Like they say in the movies, I was thinking.

Just like they say in the movies.

10

I AWOKE the next morning about seven and for several moments lay motionless in bed, blinking at the ceiling. I was aware that the muscles of my arms and legs ached and that my throat was dry and raw. I knew that feeling. It was the ravages of a sustained fear and depression. Some men got ulcers, others got the shakes or drank. I ached.

And my head was throbbing violently. I'd finally fallen asleep about 3 A.M., after drinking three half-full glasses of bourbon. Now I had a hangover. Next time, I'd get a prescription for sleeping pills.

Next time . . .

I couldn't even smile at the preposterous thought.

I got out of bed, stumbled into the bathroom and took three asperin tablets. Then, leaning on the washbasin, I looked at myself in the mirror.

My beard was dark against pale skin, sickly looking. Beneath my eyes the flesh was stained with the faint purple of fatigue, and I needed a haircut. For the last two days, following Faith Hanson, I'd badly needed a haircut.

Who was the gangster they'd killed in New York, in the barber's chair? Clearly I could recall the pictures. They'd laid out the corpse on the floor of the barbershop, with the bloodstained barber's sheet covering him.

I looked at my watch. Already, it was seven twenty. Somehow I'd spent twenty minutes, lying in bed, then taking asperin and now staring at myself in the mirror. I'd wasted twenty minutes.

Hastily I laid out my razor and shaving soap, aware that now I felt more frightened, more alone, than I had following the attack on Monday night. Perhaps it was because the attack had been anonymous: a dark, disembodied gun barrel, moving in the night, silently. But there was nothing vague about Sabella's threats. If I told Russo about the conversation in Charlene's apartment, I'd get both legs broken. Both legs.

Had Carrigan really gone?

On Sunday, he'd told me to call a special number, ask for him and identify myself as a "friend from Portland." This was Thursday. Carrigan had checked out Monday night. Had he gone back to Sacramento?

I rinsed my face, dried myself and quickly combed my hair. He'd given me the telephone number on a small slip of perforated paper. I'd put it in my wallet—in the stamp compartment. Negligently.

Fumbling, I took up my wallet from the bedside table, opening it. The paper was still inside. I glanced at my watch. Seven thirty. Without doubt, no one would answer the CIIB phone until eight thirty, possibly nine. At least an hour to wait. And at that moment Sabella could be on his way—Sabella and another man. He'd bring another man with him.

I pulled on my trousers. I must get out of the room. In the hotel lobby, I could simply refuse to go with them. A newspaperman I'd known had once stood his ground in the waiting room of a bus terminal while four hoods tried to get him out into their car. For almost an hour he'd simply sat, staring at them until a policeman had come on his routine rounds.

I'd often thought of getting a gun. Except that Larsen had always said a gun gets you shot, while . . .

Larsen.

I could phone Larsen, from a pay station, and . . .

And what?

What could I tell him? That I'd got myself caught in the middle, as he'd predicted? That he should call the Los Angeles police, on my behalf? Beyond all doubt, if I called the police, Russo would know within the hour.

I jammed my tie into a jacket pocket, checked my pants pocket for keys, wallet and money, then cautiously left my room. It was twenty to eight. The corridor was deserted. I walked into the lobby and went to a nearby phone booth. The CIIB number didn't answer. I dialed again. Still no answer.

I walked into the coffee shop and ordered a large breakfast, asking for coffee first. My headache was less painful now, and the coffee was hot and strong. After breakfast, I could think more clearly.

As I sipped the coffee, waiting to be served, I forced myself to inventory my situation, dispassionately. Two gangsters had threatened me. But of the two, Russo's actual threat was merely a refusal to protect me from Sabella. And Sabella's threat could have been more bluff than substance. He's said it himself: newspapermen and

162

police have special immunity. Killing a gangster, or a whore or even a grafting politician was one thing—a family matter. Killing someone like me or breaking my legs was something else. The Outfit craved anonymity; thus the press's special immunity. The attempt on my life could even have been a bluff—a warning.

I pushed my empty cup forward, signaling for the waitress. She was a small, trim brunette with a narrow waist and a high bosom. As she poured my coffee I thanked her, smiling. She merely nodded in reply, slightly raising one fine-plucked eyebrow. Watching her walk away, I decided that she probably dyed her hair.

As I sugared my coffee I stared out the window. I realized that, somehow, my fearfulness had diminished. Perhaps it was an exhaustion of the spirit, leaving me incapable of sensation. Or perhaps it was simple, rational objectivity. If I were a professional ski instructor, for instance, I would probably have already broken a leg in the line of duty. And broken legs could be splinted; broken noses could be set. Cuts healed; bruises eventually vanished.

And, besides, the *Sentinel* carried a full accident and health policy on me, with income provisions.

I was staring out at the smog-blushed sun, still low in the sky. Immediately outside the window I could see the gracefully landscaped entrance to the motel, with its long, curving drive. A bright red Mustang was turning in, traveling slowly.

Isn't he a blond kid? Russo had asked, *that drives a Mustang?*

I'd affirmed it.

Well then, he's lying.

But why? Why would he lie? And why, for that matter, would Johnny Hanson have made his strange accusation, without identifying his mother's lover? And why go only so far, then no further? Obviously, he was playing some strange, senseless game of fantasy with me. He'd denied ever seeing his father, yet he'd certainly seen him. He'd claimed to know that Russo—or at least the secret lover—was actually the murderer. Yet he couldn't, or wouldn't, document the charge—at least, not to me. And, assuming Russo was telling the truth, then Johnny Hanson had lied about never having visited the beachhouse.

But why?

Why volunteer a lie? To lie under pressure was understandable. But to lie gratuitously was strange.

My eggs were coming. The waitress now seemed less attractive—busty, perhaps, but bogus, with her thin-plucked eyebrows and pouty mouth, painted too large and too bright.

"Do you know how far the Ojai Valley is from here?" I asked her.

"About forty miles, I think. You can ask at the desk. They got a big map of the whole area."

"Thanks. Could I have more coffee, please?"

"Sure." Tentatively she smiled, probably thinking of her tip.

I drove the first twenty miles to the Midfield School with my attention constantly on the rear view mirror. Finally, though, climbing into the wooded foothills, I decided that I'd left Sabella's natural habitat behind. That night, back in town, would be my time for terror.

I arrived at Midfield about ten thirty, and was asked to

164

wait in Johnny Hanson's room while the boy was notified that he had a visitor. Remembering dormitory etiquette from my college days, I left the door to Johnny Hanson's room partially ajar.

The room was small and cramped. Books, papers and clothing littered the desk, the bed and the single easy chair. Gingerly I removed a sweater and jacket from the chair and sat down to wait—deciding not to smoke, since I saw no ashtray. Instead, looking around the room, I tried to form some impression of the occupant, I looked first for photographs, and on the desk saw a portfolio-type double picture frame. On one side was a single studio photograph of Mrs. Hanson. She was unsmiling and wore a simple black dress and single strand of pearls. She looked lovely, intelligent and unapproachable. On the other side of the frame was a carefully cropped montage of informal snapshots, each depicting John Hanson and his son. There were fishing scenes, zoo pictures, graduation snaps and Boy Scout shots—clowning pictures and squinting-in-the-sun pictures. The father and the son made a warm, handsome pair, and their family resemblance was plain. I reached over for the picture frame, intending to study the father's face for traces of weakness or despair. But just as I stretched out my arm I heard a sound behind me. Turning, I saw Johnny Hanson standing in the doorway. His left hand still rested on the doorknob; in his right hand he held a student's looseleaf binder and two textbooks. His face showed no surprise; his posture betrayed neither uneasiness nor uncertainty.

For a long, silent moment we simply stared. Then, slowly, I rose to my feet. Yet I was hardly conscious of having made the movement. Because, in that single in-

165

stant, the figure before me stood in a different setting, beyond the present place and time. He had come covertly from some obscure periphery; he stood silhouetted against a black velvet darkness of the night, listening—watching silently. Waiting. He was . . .

". . . Mr. Drake, isn't it?" he was saying.

"Yes, I—— How are you, Johnny? I hope you don't mind my coming. I . . ." Somehow, I couldn't say any more.

He came a few paces into the room, swinging the door shut behind him. Then, with a single practiced teen-age gesture he tossed his books on the bed and cleared a place to sit down.

"After I talked to you last Sunday, thinking about it, I decided that you'd probably want to talk to me again." His voice was low but distinct.

With an effort I looked at Johnny Hanson directly, trying to assess him.

"Why did you think I'd want to talk to you?"

He didn't answer immediately. His eyes were filmed with the fixed, glassy sheen of a quiet, almost imperceptible insanity. The eyes now seemed part of a rigid, immobile mask, one that would surely be shattered by a single smile or dissolved by a single tear.

"Why did you think I'd want to talk to you?" I asked again.

"Because, Mr. Drake, some of the things I told you were wrong. So I felt that, if you found out, you might be back to see me." He gestured with a listless hand. He seemed to have lost interest in the conversation.

"Mother says you're a clairvoyant," he said finally. "She says you're actually quite famous." His manner seemed

166

merely polite—as if he were making desultory conversation to put me at ease.

I nodded, saying nothing—holding his gaze.

"I don't believe in ESP." His tone lacked both inflection and animation. It was almost as if he were speaking by rote or from a shallow trance.

"I'm not sure whether I believe in it either," I answered. "It's hard to believe in something you don't understand, even if it happens to you. However——" I paused, for emphasis. "However, it works."

"Oh? Does it?" The question was delivered with an arch, artificial inflection.

"Yes, it works, Johnny."

"Then I suppose you know who it was that killed Dominic Vennezio." It was said without even the smallest trace of hesitation. If anything, it was I who felt uncertain as I said:

"Yes, I think I do know who killed him."

"And that's why you're here."

"Yes. That's why I'm here."

"You think I—know something about it."

"Yes, I think you do. Or, rather, I think I know something about the murder, now. I think I know why you told me you'd never been to the beachhouse, when actually you had. I think I know why you denied seeing your father during the past year, when actually you had. And I also think I know why you told me that it was your mother's lover who murdered Vennezio."

In a total, motionless silence we stared at each other. He sat on the littered bed with his long legs crossed and his elbow resting on one knee, his cupped hand beneath his chin.

"I suppose," he said, "that I could get a lawyer to sue you for defamation of character, or harassment or something. Questioning someone about murder might be a shock that could damage him. For life."

"I know. But if I'm right, then it's something I have to do, whether I like it or not."

"Why?" He seemed merely curious, not really involved.

"Because we can't live in a society where murderers are allowed to go free."

He smiled. "That sounds pretty pompous, Mr. Drake. And it doesn't make much sense. either. There're probably a hundred murderers free right this minute, in the city of Los Angeles alone. Look at Dominic Vennezio." As he pronounced the name, I saw the first flaw appear in the mask: a spasmodic twitching of the lips, instantly controlled.

"That doesn't change anything, though," I replied. "We still can't allow murderers to go free if we can help it. And I think I can help it."

He nodded, almost indifferently. It was as though he were conceding some small point in a trivial, meaningless argument.

"After you leave here," he said, "what will you do?"

"That depends on you, Johnny."

"Mother said you're working for Russo."

"Well, that—that's right in one way and wrong in another."

"Either way," he said, "you don't look like you're feeling very virtuous about it." He rose to his feet, to stand briefly looking down at me. He seemed sunk in a deep reverie. Then, sighing with a petty, pouty exasperation, he turned away, walking with his long, graceful stride to the desk. He bent down, opened the bottom drawer and reached inside, then straightened, holding two large books in his hands. He closed the drawer with his knee, and placed the two books on the desk top. For a moment he stood pensively gazing down at the books. Then, once more sighing, he moved the top book aside, unopened. The second book was larger than the first, and by turning my head I could read the title: *Principles of Life Drawing*.

With a deliberate, almost ceremonious gesture he raised the cover. The book had been hollowed out; inside lay a small automatic pistol. He picked up the pistol and turned to face me fully, at the same time closing the book. The pistol was pointed at my chest. Now he moved across the room to lock the door, still holding the pistol on me. Then he returned to the bed, sitting as before.

Five feet separated us, possibly six.

Only once before had I ever faced a gun. I could still remember that sick sensation: staring fascinated at the round black muzzle—helplessly, incredibly afraid.

He was speaking quietly:

"I could kill you during the lunch hour, when everyone's at the dining hall. Do you have a car?"

"Wha—what?"

"I said," he repeated patiently, "do you have a car?"

"Y—yes."

He nodded. "I could kill you during the lunch hour," he repeated, musing dreamily, "and then I could get your keys. Later tonight I could drive your car up just outside the window—" he pointed to the large casement window opening directly on a graveled driveway, "—and I could load your body inside." He seemed to think about it, calculating. "I'd probably have a fairly good chance. I could make it look like an accident."

I'd been staring at the window, draped in a gauzy linen. I realized that no one passing outside could see into the room, unless a lamp were lit. I realized, too, that Johnny Hanson had already considered this possibility.

Could I suddenly kick out, for the gun? I'd heard occasional voices in the hallway outside. He might not dare to shoot.

Should I leap for him?

No. He could pull the trigger before I cleared the chair. It was the one caution the police were constantly preaching: don't startle a man with a gun. Stay quiet, stay calm. If possible, get your man talking. You can't outrun a bullet—or outfight a man with a gun.

If only I could smoke a cigarette. If only . . .

". . . did you happen to come here, anyhow?" he was saying.

"Wha—what?"

"I said," he repeated, now with a faintly impatient exasperation, "how did you happen to come here, anyhow? Was it really ESP, or what?"

As I answered, I moved to a more erect posture in the soft chair, then inched toward the cushion's edge.

"You could call it ESP," I said.

"Sit back, Mr. Drake."

I obeyed. As I did, I was aware that my shirt was damp with perspiration.

"Tell me," he insisted, "why you came here."

"I talked to your father, for one thing. And to—other people."

"My father."

"Yes."

His eyes began to blink rapidly, their fixed, glassy film shattered, revealing a deep, desperate wound within. It was the mask's second flaw, uglier and more decisive than the first.

"You didn't know, then." It was a harsh whisper. "Not for sure."

I shook my head. "No, I didn't know. I suspected. But I didn't know."

Sadly he smiled. He lowered the pistol until it rested in his lap. He looked down at the gun.

"You might've gone back to Los Angeles and never known."

"No. When I first saw you, here, I knew."

"You guessed," he said, still staring down at the gun. "You didn't know."

I was too numbed to reply. Helplessly, as it had last night, my mind began revolving in wild, eccentric circles around something Larsen had said:

You're like a kid playing blindman's buff.

Had Larsen predicted that I might be killed? Somehow it seemed desperately important that I remember—yet I couldn't. I could only . . .

"When I was six or seven," he was saying, "I can remember going to the park with my father. We used to play hide and seek. He never cared what people thought. He used to run with me and play tag." He deeply sighed. His head was still bowed. He was holding the gun very loosely now in his right hand. With his left forefinger, slowly, he begin stroking the gun. The gesture had an odd, hypnotic compulsion. His caress was gentle: almost

171

a lover's touch.

"She hated him," he said suddenly. "She killed him."

"Killed him?" A sensation of shocked disbelief penetrated the numbing helplessness of my fear. "Is he dead?"

"No, he's not dead. He's still alive. But he's dying. His soul is dying. For two years, he's been slowly dying, inside. He's a—a bum, now. A drunken bum. He was arrested a few months ago for stealing a bottle of muscatel wine from a grocery store. He went to the county jail for thirty days. Then, in jail, he couldn't stand it, without liquor, and he—he cracked up. Went insane. They sent him to the county hospital, to the psycho ward. When they were ready to release him, they told him that he had cirrhosis of the liver and that he'd die if he kept on drinking. And then they gave him his clothes and told him to go." He stopped speaking, staring down at the treasured gun. "That's why it was so easy to kill Vennezio," he said softly.

"Did your mother know you'd seen your father?" I asked.

"Are you kidding?" It was a teen-ager's expression, grotesquely incongruous. "I ask my mother to please pass the toast on Sundays—and once in a while I do her the favor of asking for money. But that's all—everything. After sixteen years, all I can think about is subtle little ways to make her life miserable. It—it's an obsession. A total obsession. I think about her constantly, planning what I'll do to her next—how I can make her suffer, while I still seem to be a dutiful, devoted son. I suppose, really, killing Mr. Vennezio was a kind if an—extension of that same planning. It—it had the same feeling, plan-

172

ning to kill him. There was the same feeling that everything else was unreal and far away—everything else but the planning."

"When did you decide to kill him?"

He frowned, thinking about it. Then he answered matter-of-factly, "about two months ago. Maybe a little longer."

I must have almost smiled as I said, "You certainly had a lot of people fooled. Almost everyone thought it was a professional job."

"When you don't care about being punished," he said slowly, "then there's nothing to worry about. I can remember standing looking down at him. I could still smell the powder smoke. And I remember thinking that I'd been a lot more frightened as a kid, watching horror movies. I didn't feel a thing. I wasn't frightened, and I wasn't hysterical. I wasn't angry, and I wasn't glad—I didn't laugh, and I didn't cry. I was just standing there."

"How'd you happen to phone the police?"

He looked at me. "You seem to be fairly perceptive, Mr. Drake. Can't you figure that out?"

"I imagine that you wanted them to arrive while your mother was there."

"Yes." He nodded gravely. "That's exactly right."

"Did you want to involve her in the murder?"

"No. I wanted to shame her. I couldn't forget my father, in that psycho ward. It's all I could think about. I couldn't sleep, thinking about it." As he spoke, his manner again became withdrawn, his tone again dreamily monotonous. "I've often thought, since, that the weeks I spent planning the murder were . . . He paused, searching for the word. "Exhilarating. It's the only time I can remember feeling alive. Really alive."

"How *did* you plan the murder?"

"It all started with a gardener we had here at the school. He was an eccentric, paranoid old man, and he only lasted a week or so. But he had several guns. Pistols. That's one of the reasons he was fired, because he wouldn't give up his guns. Anyhow, one day I was doing some sketching close to his little cottage. It was probably a week after I'd seen Dad, and already I was trying to think of some way I could kill Vennezio. It was mostly fantasy, of course—but the more I thought about it, the more the idea seemed to take on substance. So, when I saw that the gardener had been called to take a phone message down by the gate, I simply walked inside his cottage. I'm not sure I was even looking for a gun—at least not consciously. In fact, I remember that I was surprised to find myself inside the cottage. But there it was—" He lifted the small automatic, fondly. "—lying on a table. So I simply picked it up, put it in my pocket and walked out."

"What'd you do next?"

"Well, next, I began to plan it all in detail. I thought of several plans, of course. That was the worse part, in fact —trying to make up my mind between two or three alternatives. But finally I decided to do it on a Sunday night when I'd be visiting Mother. And after I decided, it all seemed to fall into place. It was all so simple, really. I just drove off Sunday night about 6:30, ostensibly going back to school, as usual. I knew that, about an hour later, she'd leave for the beachhouse. I'd followed her, you see. I knew. So I just drove out to the beachhouse, ahead of her. I got there just a little after seven thirty, as I remember. And

I . . ." His voice drifted off. He seemed sunk in some private reverie. His eyes were shining, his lips slightly parted.

"I knocked on the door," he continued, staring far beyond me. "And I heard his footsteps coming."

"Did he open the door immediately?"

"Oh, no." He seemed primly shocked. "No, no. He asked who it was, then he looked at me through the peephole. At first, I'd thought about shooting him through that peephole. I read a story, in fact, where that happened. But, this way, it was so much better. I had the gun in my right-hand jacket pocket. He let me in, of course. I said I had a message from Mother, and he let me in. I pretended to be worried; I think he was afraid of an accident. Anyhow, he let me in. And as soon as he did, I took out the gun. I—I'll never forget his expression, when he saw it." Deliciously, Johnny Hanson almost seemed to hug himself. "His eyes became absolutely like saucers. It's a cliché, I know. But it's true."

"Then you shot him."

He nodded. "Yes, I shot him. Three times. Without more than a second's pause between shots. I remember being extremely conscious of time. It seemed as if every second was an eternity—another cliché. I don't know whether you've ever smoked pot, but that was the sensation: the essence of being high. It was the end of everything—the absolute end. I remember, firing the third shot, that I felt as if I could die, right then. I realized that I'd never feel any more completely alive than I felt right at that moment."

"Then what did you do?" I asked. There was something in his macabre ecstasy that I couldn't endure—yet

175

which was completely absorbing.

"I left," he said. "I left and got in the car and drove back down the road. It was precisely eight o'clock, I remember, when I phoned the police."

"And then you drove to school."

He nodded.

"Then what?"

"Then I replaced the gun in the book—" He gestured toward the desk. "—and I got a good night's sleep. No nightmares. Nothing whatever unusual. Except that, the next morning, I remember waking early—you know, like you do sometimes on special occasions. Christmas, or your birthday. I remember lying in bed and wondering whether I'd committed the perfect crime. I didn't really think I had, of course. I wasn't that naïve. But I knew I'd come close. And . . ." He looked at me with a kind of fond vexation. "And until now, of course, it *was* the perfect crime. It could still be, with luck." He looked down at the gun and then glanced at his wristwatch. "I think I'll wait until about twelve thirty," he said. "Or maybe quarter to one." For a moment he gazed at me with a dreamy, faraway look. "I'll hate to do it, really. You seem like a gentle man, Mr. Drake. That may have been the reason I didn't hit you with the pellet gun, Monday. Subconsciously, I might not have wanted to. . . ."

Glass shattered; wood splintered. Two uniformed policemen were threshing in the curtains like fish caught in a net. *Keystone cops,* I remember thinking. *Slapstick.* Carrigan stood in the doorway, gun in hand trained at the boy still sitting on the bed—still with his legs crossed. Carrigan's voice was deep and calm; his eyes were steady.

176

"Drop it, Johnny. Right now. On the floor."

The policemen were inside the room now. A ribbon of blood flecked one policeman's hand. Splintered glass littered the floor. Their guns, too, were trained on the slight blond boy.

"Drop it," Carrigan repeated, still in the same calm, deep voice. I was helpless in my chair, watching. I was shaking violently.

The gun in the boy's hand was moving—deliberately raised up, away from his lap.

"Don't be a damn fool. *Drop it.*"

But still the gun moved—steadily, inexorably. The muzzle was pointed toward the wall adjoining my chair. Now the muzzle was moving up toward the ceiling, describing a slow, sure arc.

"Johnny. No. Please." It was my own voice.

The muzzle was now coming down toward the blond head.

"Johnny. Don't. You . . ."

The shot was muffled. The gun slipped to the floor. The body was slack, falling upon the bed. The clear blue eyes were staring directly into mine. A bright thread of blood flowed slowly down the pale, twitching cheek.

I wrenched out of the chair, stumbled and fell against the wall. Clutching my stomach with both hands, I began to vomit.

11

"ANOTHER ONE?" Larsen held the coffeepot poised over my empty cup.

"No, thanks."

For the past several moments we'd been sitting silently. It had taken me almost twenty minutes to tell Larsen the whole story. Not once had he interrupted, either to comment or to question. Now, quietly, he said:

"It's not your fault, you know. Someone would've found out. And he still would've killed himself."

"No one can say that for sure. Besides, who would've found out?"

"Carrigan," he answered promptly. "Carrigan is an easy guy to underestimate. But you can take my word for it: he'd've found out. After you phoned yesterday I did some checking, just out of curiosity. And I discovered that Carrigan had been assigned to the Vennezio murder. Very quietly. He was working completely alone, as I understand it, so as to protect himself from any kind of political pressure or local interference."

"Maybe he'd've found out, maybe not. But no one'll ever know whether the kid would've killed himself."

"Do you think Mrs. Hanson knew the boy was guilty?" he asked, obviously to change the subject.

"I don't know," I answered. "I think she might've guessed."

He nodded thoughtfully. Then, lightly bantering, he asked, "Did you get the rest of your money?"

"Not yet."

"Did you ask for it?"

"I already told you: I just got back to the motel and packed my bag and left. No phone calls, nothing. I even forgot my toilet kit and my dirty laundry."

"In other words, Russo didn't know whether you'd left town or not."

"I'm sure he knew. But I didn't tell him."

"What're you going to do, send Aidia Vennezio a bill or something?"

"I suppose so." Wryly I smiled. "I've still got time. It's not the end of the month."

Larsen smiled in return and poured himself a cup of coffee.

"Well," he said finally, "I think you're very, very lucky. Of all the conceivable combinations of all the people who might've killed him, for all the possible reasons, it couldn't've worked out better for you. You might not even be sitting here right now if it had turned out to be Russo or Sabella or Mrs. Vennezio's dwarf, not to mention Angelo. And, as far as that's concerned, I don't think anything but the boy's suicide would've done you much good, either. I'm completely convinced that, once you discovered the murderer's identity and told Russo, he'd've ordered you to get on the plane for San Francisco and not to tell a living soul."

179

"I suppose you're right." I began gathering up my cigarettes and matches. I knew Larsen was anxious to get back to fiber-glassing his boat. And confirming the thought, Larsen rose to his feet with me, leaving his coffee half-finished.

"What I still can't figure out," he said as we walked out into the back yard, "is why Johnny would've volunteered all that information in the first place—about knowing who the murderer was, then refusing to identify him, yet still insisting he knew. It's very strange. It was so contradictory that it was sure to arouse suspicion eventually."

"I think it's got something to do with the criminal's urge to confess. I've heard you talk about that often—like in *Crime and Punishment,* which I understand psychologists still quote as a classic example."

Thoughtfully Larsen nodded. "You could be right. Bravado—the so-called superman complex—is really just the other side of the urge to confess. Like leaving evidence, unconsciously. That happens all the time."

"There's something else, too, about Johnny's so-called tip to me. He identified the murderer as his mother's secret lover. Yet, thinking about it, I'm not completely sure that he knew Russo was even involved with his mother."

"But Russo said that he'd seen Johnny out at the beach cabin."

"Yes, but Johnny didn't see Russo. And, what's more, it wouldn't proven anything if he had seen him. They were just two guys in two cars, parked beside the ocean." I shook my head. "It doesn't add up, that way. I think Johnny might've had a feeling that she had another lover, but I don't think he was sure."

"Well, obviously, he thought he'd divert suspicion from

180

himself if he named another suspect."

"Maybe so," I replied doubtfully. "But you said it yourself: coming out with it like he did, so strangely, he'd've been better off to've kept quiet."

"How do you figure it, then?"

"I figure," I said slowly, "that, again, it was a kind of an unconscious confession. He was naming his mother's secret lover as the murderer—which was, in fact, the unconscious truth. He was naming himself."

Larsen sighed. "The faithful old Oedipus complex. I'll be glad when it goes out of style. The way it is now, everything's so predictable. Besides, I thought you said the kid was queer."

"That was just an impression. He was screwed up, obviously. And, as far as that goes, Oedipus and homosexuality are supposed to be pretty close."

Larsen nodded. Obviously, he was losing interest in the conversation. "I wonder," he said musingly, "how things'll work out with Russo and Sabella."

"I figure Sabella'll get transferred to the Des Moines office. At least."

Larsen smiled, and we stood in silence for a moment.

"You want any help fiber-glassing?" I asked.

"No, thanks." He smiled and clapped me lightly on the shoulder. "Besides, you need a vacation. If I were you, I'd take off for a long weekend. Go down to Carmel or somewhere."

"If I could find someplace where I didn't have to stay in a motel," I replied, "maybe I would."

"I see what you mean." Again he smiled, said good-bye and turned toward the garage.

I got into my car and drove slowly away, aimlessly. I

switched on the radio and found some loud rock music, but the noise didn't help. I couldn't forget the bright ribbon of blood trickling down the pale, twitching cheek— and the eyes that seemed still alive, staring into mine.